Mustang Meadow

Redemption Mountain,
Book Twenty-Three

Historical Western Romance

SHIRLEEN DAVIES

Books Series by Shirleen Davies

Historical Western Romances

Redemption Mountain
MacLarens of Fire Mountain Historical
MacLarens of Boundary Mountain

Contemporary Western Romance

Cowboys of Whistle Rock Ranch
MacLarens of Fire Mountain Contemporary
Macklins of Whiskey Bend

Romantic Suspense

Eternal Brethren Military Romantic Suspense
Peregrine Bay Romantic Suspense

The best way to stay in touch is to subscribe to my newsletter. Visit my Website *www.shirleendavies.com* and fill in your email and name in the Join My Newsletter boxes. That's it!

Mustang Meadow is a work of fiction. Names, characters, places, and incidents are either products of the author's imagination or used fictitiously. Any resemblance to actual events, locales, or persons, living or dead, is wholly coincidental.

Cover design by Sweet 'n Spicy Designs

ISBN: 978-1-947680-99-9

I care about quality, so if you find something in error, please contact me via email at
shirleen@shirleendavies.com

Description

As frontier Montana rages with felons and floods,
Their hearts wage the greatest battle.

Sean MacLaren is ready for the challenges awaiting him in Splendor, Montana. As the town's first veterinarian, he must overcome doubt, fear, and distrust to convince local ranchers to give his skills a try. It's a tricky proposition, hampered by his growing affection for a certain outspoken New York socialite determined to shove her way into town business.

Camilla Santori broke from her formal, controlling east coast life to join her brother in the wild frontier of Montana. She's determined to make her mark in the growing town while keeping her attraction to the new veterinarian a carefully guarded secret. Not only is he nine years younger, his manner and speech are too, well...western.

As multiple dangers plague the opinionated, yet guileless woman, Sean finds he can't allow her to navigate the threats alone. Nor can he stop her from getting involved in the numerous crises confronting the town.

When a fast-moving sickness threatens the burgeoning cattle industry, Sean finds himself relying on Camilla to help him bring an end to the terrible scourge. In the process, their affection grows, pushing their frail friendship to its limit.

Will the continued threats to Camilla, and the town, draw them together? Or will challenging events drive a wedge between the taciturn vet and the strong-willed lady from the east?

Mustang Meadow, book twenty-three in the Redemption Mountain historical western romance series, is a full-length, clean and wholesome novel with an HEA and no cliffhanger

Mustang Meadow

Chapter One

MacLaren Ranch
Splendor, Montana
Spring 1874

The wild mustang reared up with a shrill whinny, hooves clawing at the air as Thane MacLaren clung to the saddle. His hat flew off as the horse twisted in a violent attempt to dislodge its unwanted rider. Thane gritted his teeth, gripping the reins tighter as the mustang bucked and kicked.

"Easy now, easy," Thane said in a low, soothing voice, even as the horse continued to fight against him. He could feel the powerful muscles bunching and flexing beneath him as the mustang put all its strength into throwing him off.

It was no use. Thane had been tossed from more horses than he could count over the years, but he wasn't some greenhand recruit. He knew how to stick on a bucker, and he wasn't about to let this wild one best him.

With a final furious blow of unease and his ears pinned back, the mustang twisted, going rigid, all four legs planted stubbornly on the ground. Thane didn't relax his white-knuckled grip, waiting to see if the horse would explode into another round of bucking. When he remained still, sides heaving, Thane loosened the reins and leaned forward to pat the mustang's sweat dampened neck.

"There now, that wasn't so bad."

The mustang flicked an ear but stayed put. Thane kept up the gentle stream of nonsense words, keeping his voice low and calm. He felt some of the tension leave the horse's body. The mustang still trembled, but the fight had gone out of him for now. Thane knew it wasn't over yet. Breaking a wild one took time and patience. But this was a start.

Satisfaction welled up in Thane as he sat astride the exhausted mustang. This one would make a fine cow pony once properly trained. The horse had spirit and endurance—qualities to be valued. With care and handling, the wildness could be shaped into loyalty.

Thane smiled to himself. This was what he loved. Thane had an innate sense to understand the potential beneath the rough exterior. Given time, even the most contrary horse could become a trusted partner. All it took was perseverance. And of that, Thane had plenty.

Sean MacLaren leaned against the corral fence, arms folded across his chest as he watched his cousin work with the wild mustang. Though he'd spent the last few years immersed in his veterinary studies in Edinburgh, it felt good here on the ranch. The wide open Montana sky, the smell of horses and leather, the creak of saddle leather. This was home, as much as the ranch he'd grown up on in California.

As his cousin coaxed the horse to walk a few steps, Sean studied his strong, lanky build. He'd shot up in height since Sean left for university. Thane still had the determined set to his jaw he remembered. The look saying Thane would stick to a task no matter how many times he was thrown off and had to remount.

Sean grinned, recalling the day at the California ranch when Thane had been tossed into the horse trough trying to break his first colt. Even sopping wet, he'd climbed right back on the horse. Tenacity like that would serve Thane well out here breaking mustangs.

Letting his gaze travel over the vast ranch, Sean felt the familiar swell of wonder and excitement. The ranch covered rugged hills and wooded draws. It was beautiful, open country, filled with possibilities.

"Beautiful, aye?" Bram's voice broke Sean's reverie, and he turned to see his cousin standing beside him. Bram had a slight Scottish lilt that always made Sean smile.

"Stunning." He nodded toward the landscape. "I can see why you all love it out here so much."

Bram grinned. "Aye. It gets under your skin."

"It does. I'm not sure I could handle the isolation for long."

"That's part of the appeal." Bram's eyes sparkled. "You learn to rely on yourself out here. And your family, of course."

Soon, he'd be opening his veterinary practice in Splendor. The thought sent a spike of anticipation through him. He was ready to put his training to use, to carve out a new life here on the frontier. He'd yet to tell his cousins of his decision.

It wouldn't be easy, but challenges had never stopped him from pursuing his dreams. With his cousins' ranch flourishing, and him serving the community as a veterinarian, the future held great promise.

Thane managed to get the wild mustang under control, bringing the horse to the fence, where Sean and Bram watched.

"He's got some fight in him yet. I think he'll make a fine cow pony once he's broke." Thane patted the horse's muscular neck.

Sean nodded, a grin appearing. "You've always had a special way with the horses."

Bram nodded. "Aye, the lad does."

Thane grinned, reveling in his older brother's praise. Though they shared ownership of the ranch, Bram was the one with the most experience.

"Couldn't have done it without all you've taught me." Thane looked at Bram, then over at Sean. "Suppose you'll be putting those veterinary skills to use before long, patching up whatever critters we drag in."

"I'm happy to help any way I can."

Thane and Bram had welcomed him onto the ranch like a third brother. Both had assumed he'd help with chores when not tending to injured or sick animals.

Bram chuckled. "Once word spreads about your skills, folks from all over will be coming to the ranch, asking for your help. You'll be the only educated vet in the entire territory."

Sean hoped Bram was right. He wanted to make his own imprint, not just ride on the coattails of his cousins' success. Montana was a place to prove himself.

He gazed out at the endless Montana horizon. This wide open space was different from the large family ranch the three men had grown up on. There was a wildness to this land that called to his adventurous spirit.

"Remember when we were kids, and you'd beg your ma to let you be the one to break the colts?" Sean asked, smiling at the memory. "You've come a long way from those days."

Thane chuckled. "I was too cocky back then. Nearly got myself killed a few times trying to prove I was as good as everyone else. Especially Bram." He patted the neck of the bay mustang. "Now I understand it takes patience and empathy. You've got to earn the horse's trust."

Bram walked closer to the gelding, looking him over. "Aye, he's learned when brute force won't work, you need a gentle hand," Bram added. Though the brothers' personalities differed, with Bram being bolder and Thane more soft-spoken, they balanced each other out.

Sean admired the way Thane had grown into a confident horseman without losing his thoughtful nature. He hoped veterinary school had honed his own skills and instincts without dampening his compassion for animals.

"I can't wait to see you put all that book learning to use," Thane told Sean, as if reading his cousin's mind.

Sean smiled, warmed by his cousin's faith in him.

Sean stepped outside, inhaling a deep breath early the next morning, his gaze moving to the barn and corrals. Though he loved his family's ranch, it no longer felt like the frontier. Here, the frontier still beckoned with opportunity and challenge. He stepped back inside, facing his cousins as they ate breakfast.

"I've decided to open a veterinary practice in Splendor."

Thane's eyes widened. "Truly?"

Sean nodded, a grin spreading across his face. "It's the perfect place to forge my own path, apart from the MacLaren legacy. There's cattle, horses, sheep, pigs, ranch dogs, and frontier folk in need of a vet. I can make a real impact."

"Leave it to you to pick the most rough-and-tumble town in these parts." Bram shook his head with a chuckle.

"It won't be easy, I know. But I'm ready for whatever comes. This is my chance to test myself, to put all I've learned into practice." His green eyes shone with resolve.

Thane clasped Sean's shoulder. "We believe in you, cousin. Just try not to get yourself shot by rowdy cowboys, eh?"

Sean laughed. "I'll do my best. With luck, I can earn their trust, just like with breaking a wild horse."

Unlike most in his large, extended family, Sean's heart yearned for new experiences, new challenges. Splendor awaited, rough and full of potential. Similar to an unbroken mustang. He poured a cup of coffee, turning toward his cousins.

"California was comfortable, predictable. I didn't become a vet just to follow the easy path." He met their eyes, his jaw set. "I want to test myself, prove I can survive on my own. Demonstrate how the skills I've developed will matter out here."

Thane nodded. "We understand, Sean. This wild land gets into your blood. You gotta follow your dreams."

"Just promise you'll visit often." Bram stood. "It won't be the same around here without you."

Sean clasped Bram's shoulder. "Wild horses couldn't keep me away. You're my family."

Bram pulled him into a quick, tight hug. As they parted, emotion shone in his eyes as his cousins walked off to start their work for the day.

Alone again, he took a deep breath, steeling himself for the journey ahead. Failure was possible, even likely. But he refused to let fear stop him from trying.

The following morning, Sean said goodbye to his cousins and their wives. He turned his horse west, toward the impressive mountain range and his future in Splendor.

The short distance passed in solitude as Sean lost himself in thought. He reflected on the path that led him here, to this pivotal moment. Years of intense study, late nights poring over medical texts, the nonstop training to hone his veterinary skills. All of it was for this—to bring his knowledge to a town in need.

A hawk's piercing cry jolted him from his reverie. He surveyed the lonely terrain. The sheer scale of it made him feel small, yet filled him with awe. This was a land of extremes. Harsh and unforgiving, but possessing a stark, natural beauty.

Sean continued west. Bram had told him the trip wasn't long if he kept heading toward the large mountain range. In the distance, dark clouds were gathering, promising rain. He frowned, hoping to reach Splendor before the downpour.

A rumble of thunder echoed across the plains.

Urging his horse into a trot, he scanned the landscape for any sign of cover. In the distance, he spotted a small cabin nestled in a copse of trees. Guiding his mount off the trail, he approached the spare homestead as the first raindrops began to fall.

Dismounting, Sean led his horse to the cabin's overhang. When he was about to knock, the door opened to reveal an elderly woman, her face creased with age, her eyes sharp.

"Saw you from the window. Reckoned you'd be looking for shelter. C'mon in and dry off."

Thanking her, Sean introduced himself before stepping inside the humble cabin. The woman busied herself stoking the fire as he shed his wet slicker.

"Name's Ida. Some people call me Widow Ida. There's coffee on the stove if you want it. Help yourself."

"Sean MacLaren. I'm on my way to Splendor."

Over steaming mugs of coffee, Ida asked Sean about himself. He explained his plans to open a veterinary practice in Splendor.

"Good folk there. My husband and I lived there years back. We had ourselves a little spread outside town. Then he got the urge to move closer to Big Pine." Her eyes took on a faraway look, as if glimpsing the past. "It's the territorial capital east of here. Turned out, there were too many people there for my husband, so we built this cabin. I ride into Splendor every couple weeks to get supplies."

When the rain stopped, he thanked her again for the hospitality. Mounting, he started back on the trail. Not long afterward, Splendor came into view. The sight sent a thrill through him. Though he'd been there several times with his cousins, today was different.

This would be the day he'd begin a new chapter in his life.

Chapter Two

Camilla Santori gazed out the window of the Eagle's Nest restaurant, taking in the rough wood structures of her new home in Splendor, Montana. Though she'd lived a life of privilege and luxury as a wealthy heiress in New York, Camilla felt drawn to the wildness and simplicity of the west.

She was the eldest of eight children born to Reginald and Marguerite Santori, pillars of New York society. Her father had built a prosperous financial empire, which afforded the family an extravagant mansion on Fifth Avenue near Central Park, and summers spent at their sprawling estate on Long Island. As a young woman, Camilla had been groomed to marry well and maintain the family's social standing.

Yet now, at thirty-eight, she found herself seeking something beyond the confines of New York society. When her youngest brother, Cole, who was a deputy in Splendor, decided to marry Martha van Plew, Camilla made the decision to join them. She yearned for open skies and new adventures. Most of all, she hoped to find a sense of purpose which had eluded her in New York.

Splendor might not offer the comforts of home, but it represented a fresh start. She was determined to embrace this new chapter, and forge her own path separate from the Santori name. Adventure awaited in this rugged paradise she now called home.

Camilla's thoughts turned to her siblings back home. When she'd announced her intention to move west, they'd reacted with shock and disapproval.

"It's dangerous," her sister, Josephine, had fretted. "The frontier is no place for a genteel lady like yourself."

Her brother, Theodore, was more blunt. "Montana is a godforsaken wilderness full of savages and outlaws. You won't last a month out there."

Even Cole, who'd settled in Splendor himself, had cautioned her of the harsh conditions she would face.

Determined, Camilla refused to be deterred. She appreciated their concern, but felt confident she could adapt and even thrive here. After a lifetime of rigid expectations in New York, she yearned for the freedom the west promised.

So, she'd packed her bags, bid her worried family farewell, and boarded the westbound train with eager anticipation. With each mile carrying her closer to Splendor, her spirit felt lighter.

This was her bold leap into the unknown, chasing horizons called to her restless soul. She was ready to embrace whatever challenges lay ahead, determined to prove herself more resilient than her family realized.

Leaving the Eagle's Nest, Camilla gazed around the quaint, though rustic town, taking in the dirt roads, wooden storefronts, and residents going about their normal routines. Splendor was far from the gas lamps and cobblestone streets of New York.

A forceful voice called out. "Miss Santori!"

She turned to see Noah Brandt, a broad-shouldered man with a neatly trimmed beard, approach. Beside him was a beautiful woman, her stunning red hair swept up in a chignon.

"This is my wife, Abby." Noah had rented Camilla her house in town.

Camilla's smile was warm with welcome. "It's a pleasure to meet you, Abby. Please, call me Camilla."

"Wonderful," Abbie said. "If you don't mind, we'll tag along."

As they walked, Noah shared a story about him and Gabe Evans, the town sheriff and Noah's closest friend. Camilla knew the Brandts and Evans family were pillars of the community.

When they arrived at the charming single-story cottage, Camilla invited them inside, but Noah held up a hand.

"We're on our way to talk with Sean MacLaren, the new veterinarian in town."

"Well then, I can't thank you enough for renting this to me."

"We're happy to have you," Abby said. "Let us know if you need anything at all."

The next morning, Camilla was arranging some personal items around the living room when a knock sounded at the door. She opened it to find Martha, her sister-in-law, on the stoop holding a basket.

"Thought you could use some help with the new items you ordered." Martha stepped inside.

The two women worked companionably, hanging draperies and placing area rugs as they caught up on family news. Eventually, the conversation turned to the Splendor Home for Orphans.

"The children at the orphanage dearly need some extra attention," Martha explained. "With your education and background, you'd be perfect."

Camilla nodded, a purposeful glint in her eye. "Just show me where I'm needed."

This was exactly the meaningful activity she'd envisioned. The ability to use her skills to have an impact in her new town.

Later in the week, Camilla entered the town hall, eager to attend her first public meeting as a resident of Splendor. The large room was filled with townspeople, abuzz with lively debates. She spotted Martha and Cole across the room and made her way over.

"Quite a turnout this evening." Camilla took a seat beside them.

Cole gave a knowing nod. "All the new people moving in is causing some growing pains. Folks are fired up about deciding how to move forward."

Camilla surveyed the hall. The atmosphere was charged with passionate views being exchanged as the meeting got underway. This was democracy in action, even on the frontier. Camilla found herself leaning forward, listening intently to each speaker. She respected the sincerity behind every opinion, even those with which she didn't fully agree with.

When the floor opened for public comments, Camilla considered her words. Though somewhat new in town, she had a stake in Splendor's future. She stood, smoothing her skirt.

"Progress inevitably brings change," she began. "When navigating it, we must take care not to sacrifice what makes this place so special—its community, its spirit. Growth shaped with care can enrich a town. We must decide how this will be accomplished together, with open minds and good faith."

Murmurs rippled through the hall as Camilla took her seat. She'd spoken her mind without pretense, and it felt right.

Camilla's remarks sparked a vigorous discussion as others chimed in with their perspectives. Some echoed her call for balance, while others argued adamantly for either full steam ahead or resisting change at any cost.

As the debate wore on, Camilla felt compelled to speak again. She stood, gathering her thoughts before addressing the crowd.

"My friends, there are good hearts and minds on all sides here. Though we may differ in our visions, we share a love for this town and a desire to do right by it."

Camilla made eye contact with those she knew, as well as unfamiliar faces. "Rather than divide ourselves, let's find common ground. With care and compromise, we can build the future together. There is no challenge we cannot meet if we face it united as one community."

This time, her words were met with murmurs of agreement and a splatter of grumbling. Though far from solved, a spirit of cooperation was emerging from the contentious talks. Camilla sat, heart expanding with hope. If stubborn New Yorkers like her could find openness here, anything was possible. She couldn't wait to see what tomorrow would bring.

Sean had been observing the meeting from the back of the room, leaning against the wall, with his arms folded across his chest. Though he didn't know Camilla, he recognized her as the newcomer who had recently moved to town.

He watched as she spoke again, this time taking a more conciliatory tone. Admirable as her sentiments were, Sean doubted it would be so simple to unite everyone. Individuals who settled here were fiercely independent, going about their lives in whatever way they chose.

Still, he appreciated her willingness to bridge divides rather than widen them. There was courage in her conviction, even if it was tempered with naïveté.

As the meeting adjourned, Sean decided against approaching Camilla to introduce himself. It was best not to get entangled with an outsider, no matter how spirited she seemed. Touching the brim of his hat, he slipped outside into the night.

Camilla left the town hall meeting feeling invigorated. Though some of the townspeople had challenged her perspectives, she appreciated the open discourse. It was far more stimulating than the tepid conversations over tea she was accustomed to in New York. Here, people spoke their minds, and she found it refreshing.

As Camilla strolled home under a full moon, she felt a growing fondness for this rugged place and its people. Though her family insisted she wouldn't last a month out west, she was determined to prove them wrong. Splendor was precisely what she needed.

The next morning, Sean stopped by the general store to pick up supplies. Gathering his purchases, he noticed a woman perusing the canned goods section. She seemed familiar, though he couldn't place from where. Shrugging it off, he headed to the counter to pay.

Camilla read the labels on the canned goods, selecting what she needed. Glancing up, she noticed a tall, broad-shouldered man paying for his purchases. Though she only caught a glimpse of his profile, something about him seemed familiar. Then she remembered. He was the handsome stranger from the town hall meeting last night. The one who'd been standing at the back of the room. One of her neighbors had mentioned his name. What was it? Sam? No. Sean? Yes, Sean MacLaren.

She felt her cheeks flush, recalling how attractive she'd found him. Camilla had noticed him right away, listening, absorbing every word. Though he hadn't joined the debate, his sharp eyes seemed to miss nothing.

Sean tipped his hat to the shopkeeper and turned to leave. He was even more striking up close. Then she remembered. They'd met months earlier, when he'd chastised her for walking alone at night. *Sean MacLaren.*

Gathering her courage, she stepped into his path. "Excuse me. You probably don't recall meeting me earlier this winter. I'm Camilla Santori." She extended her hand in greeting.

Sean hesitated, not recalling them meeting before now, but seeing her close-up, he did remember her from the school meeting. Recovering, he shook her hand briefly.

"Sean MacLaren." His voice was a rich baritone that sent a little shiver through her. Their eyes met and held for a moment before Sean nodded and stepped around her. "I'm sorry, but I don't recall when we first met. However, I'm pleased to make your acquaintance now. If you'll excuse me, I must head out."

Camilla watched him stride out the door, butterflies swirling in her stomach. She couldn't remember the last time she'd felt such an instant attraction to someone. There was an intensity to him she found intriguing.

Shaking her head to clear it, she gathered the supplies and headed to the counter to pay. As she made small talk with the shopkeeper, her mind kept wandering back to Sean.

Stepping outside into the bright afternoon sun, she noticed him across the street. He glanced up and their eyes met before he looked away. She felt her cheeks flush again. What was it about this stoic cowboy that flustered her so?

Turning toward home, Camilla replayed their brief exchange in her mind. She was surprised and a little disappointed he hadn't been more friendly.

Still, last night, Martha had mentioned Sean was a bit of a loner, more at home with animals than people. Perhaps he was simply shy around new acquaintances.

She resolved to get to know him better when the opportunity arose. Beneath his rough exterior, she sensed a complex man with hidden depths. She wanted to understand what drove him, what kept him so isolated.

As she walked, Camilla felt a growing excitement about laying down roots here. The people were genuine, the landscape stunning. She looked forward to volunteering at the orphanage and finding her place in this community.

Most of all, she hoped to see Sean again soon. Camilla quickened her pace, eager to share details of their encounter with Martha. Changing course, she made the short walk to her brother and sister-in-law's home.

Rapping three times on the door, she entered. Martha looked up from the quilt she was mending. "Finished so soon? How did it go in town?"

Camilla removed her bonnet, her cheeks flushed. "It was wonderful. I'm starting to feel at home here." She sat down next to Martha, a serious tone to her voice. "And you'll never believe who I ran into. Sean MacLaren. What do you know about him?"

Martha thought a moment. "Not much more than I already mentioned, I'm afraid. He's new to town. You might already know he's a veterinarian. Cole told me he trained at a university in Scotland. Sean seems to keep to himself. His cousins are Bram and Thane MacLaren. Their families own a huge amount of land in northern California, where they run cattle and breed horses. The cousins own a ranch east of Splendor. Both are married to real nice women. My understanding is Sean is unencumbered." She smiled on the last.

They were quiet for a few minutes before Camilla spoke. "Well, we should be getting to the orphanage. I can't wait to start volunteering there."

Knowing the topic of Sean was closed, Martha smiled. "I'm sure those children will adore you."

Donning her bonnet, images of Sean's chiseled features and intense gaze filled her mind. She hoped they would meet again soon under better circumstances.

While Martha drove the wagon toward the orphanage, Camilla took in the sights and sounds of the bustling town. Cowboys on horseback tipped their hats as they passed. The tantalizing aroma of freshly baked bread from the bakery, mingling with the earthy scent of horses.

As Martha headed out of town, Camilla thought back to the meeting the previous night. She'd been surprised at how welcoming most of the townsfolk were to her ideas. Back in New York, her opinions were usually dismissed by male members of society. Here, her voice was heard.

Well, all except for one brooding rancher who'd stared daggers at her when she'd suggested women should be allowed more roles outside the home. The man certainly had old-fashioned ideas about a woman's place. Camilla made a mental note to avoid riling him up again if their paths crossed.

Before long, they arrived at a charming two-story house with a sweeping wraparound porch. A hand-painted sign out front read "Splendor Home for Orphans". Camilla straightened her spine and marched up the steps, alongside Martha, ready to begin her first day of volunteering.

Inside, she found a gaggle of children in the parlor. Their faces lit up when they saw Martha.

"Hello, children. Let me introduce a new volunteer. Her name is Miss Camilla. I'm certain you're going to like her."

The kids crowded around Camilla, clamoring for her attention. She laughed, thinking she could get used to this bustling place. It already felt more like home than New York ever did.

Chapter Three

Sean stood at the edge of the crowd, scanning the sea of unfamiliar faces. His gaze landed on a dark-haired woman across the way. Camilla. Their eyes locked for a brief moment before they both looked away, feigning disinterest.

Sighing, he turned his attention back to the musicians playing near the dance floor. He hadn't expected to see her here today. Their conversation at the general store had been brief, though civil.

As a New York socialite, she represented everything he'd left California to escape—pretentiousness, superficiality, and snobbery. Still, he had to admit she was pleasing to the eye in her green embroidered outfit.

Camilla kept her face turned away from Sean, busying herself with smoothing her skirt. She could feel his eyes on her and it unsettled her. The man set her teeth on edge with his stiff stature and aloof manner. Yet she couldn't deny his easy way with the townspeople intrigued her.

Rachel Pelletier noticed the furtive glances between Sean and Camilla and guessed the source of tension. Never one to shy away from a challenge, she joined Camilla.

"Don't you look lovely. The emerald green is perfect for you." She linked her arm through Camilla's. "Come, I want to introduce you to someone."

She allowed herself to be led across the busy yard, butterflies fluttering in her stomach. This was sure to be an interesting conversation.

Sean straightened his shoulders as Rachel approached with Camilla in tow. He plastered a polite smile on his face. "Good afternoon, ladies."

"Sean, I don't believe you've met Miss Camilla Santori," Rachel said. "Camilla is originally from New York, but has been living here in Splendor for some time now."

"A pleasure to meet you." Sean's response was cordial as he held Camilla's gaze.

"Likewise." She hoped her voice didn't betray her unease. Or let on they'd met before at the general store.

"Well, I'll leave you two to get acquainted." Rachel turned away, disappearing into the crowd.

The two appraised each other as an awkward silence descended between them.

Sean cleared his throat. "That's a nice outfit, Miss Santori. Though, the emerald silk seems more suited for a sophisticated evening in New York than a ranch celebration."

She bristled at the implied criticism. "Why, thank you, Mr. MacLaren. I'll take that as a compliment. We New York ladies do have a certain sense of style, even on the frontier."

Pausing, she considered her next words. "I must say, your attire seems better suited for the Scottish moors than a cattle ranch in Montana."

Sean glanced down at his tweed jacket and vest, touching the pocket watch chain. "I suppose you're right. One clings to familiarity when everything else is new and strange."

Her expression softened. "I understand. Change can be difficult." She hesitated. "I heard you're a veterinarian. You're the first educated animal doctor I've met. What made you pursue such a career?"

Sean tensed, his guard going up. He wasn't ready to reveal anything too personal. "I've always had an affinity for animals."

Sensing his reluctance, she switched tactics. "Well, veterinary skills are certainly valued here. Splendor is lucky to have you."

"Let's hope I can live up to expectations," he muttered.

Sean cleared his throat, deciding to make an effort. "The truth is, I'm passionate about veterinary medicine. I studied at the finest school in Scotland, perhaps the most noted in the world for my field, and graduated top of my class."

He glanced at Camilla to gauge her reaction. She nodded encouragement, her blue eyes attentive. "Most impressive."

"Cattle ranching is the lifeblood of towns like Splendor. Keeping livestock healthy improves the entire community's welfare. It's meaningful work."

Camilla smiled. "It seems you've found your calling."

"I hope so. My family has a long legacy in the California ranching business. I wanted to forge my own path, separate from their influence."

"It takes courage to venture into the unknown."

"What about you, Miss Santori? What prompted a New York socialite to come out west?"

She hesitated. "Let's say I sought a change from the stifling social order back home. The frontier offers more opportunities for women to spread their wings."

"Well, you certainly stand out in this crowd." Sean's eyes swept over her stylish gown.

"In a good way, I hope."

Their conversation continued, two strangers attempting to discover common ground. The differences between them seemed vast.

Camilla tilted her head, regarding Sean. "Speaking of opportunities, I'm curious to know your thoughts on Splendor's growth. As a newcomer yourself, do you think the town would benefit from more shops, businesses, perhaps a more solid framework?"

He pondered the question. "There's merit to improving Splendor. At some point, expansion could ruin its character and natural beauty. The problem is people are drawn to this town. People such as you and me." He gestured to the sweeping vista of the ranch. "Most folks here value tradition. They're wary of too much change too fast."

Her eyes sparked with interest. "An insightful perspective. Though, some change can be positive, bringing conveniences and advancement."

"A fair point." Sean sensed an engaging debate brewing. "But there's much to be said for preserving what makes a place unique. Splendor's heart is in its ranch lands and people, not grand buildings."

"True, to an extent," she countered. "But shouldn't we also look to the future? Imagine if women had more say here. We could help guide progress, and shape Splendor for the better."

He raised an eyebrow. "You make a bold proposition. Most ladies here seem content with their lot. What I mean is, those women who want a say already have the opportunity to voice their opinions."

"Opportunity is one thing. The ability to vote is quite another," Camilla declared.

His brows rose, though he refrained from being drawn into a debate on voting rights. The MacLaren women had voiced their own frustration on the subject. Most MacLaren men agreed with them.

They continued to exchange spirited opinions, both impressed by the other's knowledge and convictions. As much as they disagreed, it was an invigorating discussion.

"It's been fascinating, Dr. MacLaren." She offered a smile before leaving to join the crowd.

Sean watched Camilla from across the gathering, admiring her graceful poise as she conversed with townsfolk. He was impressed by her genuine interest in the community.

When little Emma Evans tugged her sleeve, eager to show her something, Camilla gave the girl her full attention. Sean was struck by her warmth.

Camilla continued glancing at him as he spoke with a group of men near the corral. His rugged features and muscular build cut a striking silhouette against the countryside. She noticed how the men looked at him with interest as they nodded toward a stallion.

Sean walked the corral perimeter with Dax and Luke Pelletier, pausing to inspect the horse through the fence. She watched him point to different parts of the stallion, guessing he was offering his opinion on the stallion's health and breeding potential.

They were vastly different, though each had chosen to live in the same community far away from their original homes. Hearing his concern for the community was beginning to dismantle her preconceived notions of the man. Perhaps an odd connection between her and the doctor was kindling, even if neither of them was ready to admit it.

As the afternoon wore on, dark clouds rolled in. The once clear blue sky turned ominous and foreboding. The wind picked up, whipping napkins and hats into the air.

Rachel hurried over to Camilla. "I'm afraid we're in for a storm. Most everyone is ready to head home before they're caught in the thick of it." She rushed off before Camilla could respond.

She glanced up at the threatening clouds. Across the field, she caught Sean's eye once more before he turned and strode toward the stables.

Guests scrambled, gathering children and hustling toward wagons. Camilla climbed into the Brandts' buggy just as the first fat raindrops began to fall. She had a light wrap with her, nothing heavy enough to protect her from the storm.

They rumbled down the drive as the downpour strengthened, lightning crackling in the distance. She turned around to stare through the rain at the ranch growing smaller behind them.

The rain beat down in sheets, drumming relentlessly on the buggy's black canvas top. Camilla pulled her shawl tighter around her shoulders as Noah flicked the reins, urging the horses onward down the muddy lane.

"Quite the storm," Noah shouted over his shoulder. "We'll be back in town soon enough."

Camilla nodded, teeth chattering. Beside her, Abby rubbed her own arms with brisk motions.

"Spring storms come on fast, but they clear just as quick." Abby gave her a reassuring smile.

Camilla returned a smile despite her discomfort. She was thankful for the Brandts' hospitality. As the buggy jostled down the road, the storm began to subside.

"The Pelletiers seem to be pillars of this community," she ventured. "I'm still learning the history of Splendor. How did they come to settle here?"

Noah shot a glance over his shoulder at the women. "That's quite a tale. You're right, the Pelletiers have had a big impact on shaping this town."

She settled back to listen.

"After the war ended, Dax and Luke headed out west, looking for a new start. They ended up in Texas, where they became Texas Rangers for a time. They met another Ranger named Pat Hanes. He took a liking to Dax and Luke, saw they were hard workers. When Hanes passed, he left the ranch to them. They were stunned at his decision." He paused as the buggy crossed rushing water from the rain. "Anyway, they took over Redemption's Edge and built it into one of the finest cattle operations in Montana. They're good men."

By the time they arrived in town, Camilla felt she better understood the roots and spirit of Splendor. Before he stopped in front of her house, she ventured another thought.

"The children at the orphanage are so bright and kind. They deserve good homes. I wish I could do more to help." She sighed, realizing there were no easy solutions.

Abby gave her an understanding smile. "Wish I had an answer for you. You have a generous spirit, helping out there. Those children are lucky to have you and Martha in their lives."

Noah stopped the buggy outside her house. Jumping to the ground, he helped Camilla down.

"Thank you again for the ride, and the stories. I enjoyed it very much. Especially learning more about Splendor and its people." She waved as Noah guided the buggy around a turn.

Entering her house, Camilla shook the rain from her wrap before changing out of her soaked clothes. She idly thought of Sean, dismissing the image.

There were more pressing matters than puzzling over the new vet in town. She had letters to write to the children's aid societies back east.

Seated at the writing desk, Camilla dipped the pen and began to write. There would be time enough to unravel Splendor's mysteries. Right now, her focus had to remain on the orphaned children and their futures.

Chapter Four

Thane MacLaren bent low in the saddle, urgency evident in his quick pace and determined expression. He didn't slow before reining his horse to a stop outside his cousin's house. He ran to the door, rapping his knuckles until he heard movement inside.

"I'm coming." The door opened to reveal Sean. "Thane. What brings you to town?" Sean motioned him inside.

"One of our mares is down with colic something fierce. She's in a bad way, writhing and biting at her sides."

"Is her abdomen distended?"

"Has been for hours. We've walked her, but it hasn't helped. I've never seen a horse take sick so quick."

Sean's expression grew serious as he digested the news. "Let me gather my things." He hurried to assemble his medical bag, thoughts racing through his head.

Thane shifted impatiently as Sean packed up his supplies. "Come on, we've got to hurry." Worry creased his brow at the thought of the poor horse's suffering.

Rushing outside, Thane mounted, taking the bag

Sean handed out before his cousin jumped on behind him.

"My horse is at the livery."

Soon, they were racing back to the MacLaren ranch, hoping they could get there in time to save the ailing mare. Sean's mind turned over treatment options, even as his heart went out to the animal in distress.

They pushed their horses, knowing every minute caused the mare more suffering. Galloping toward the barn, they slowed their horses. Dismounting, Sean grabbed his bag.

Bram, his wife, Selina, and Thane's wife, Sadie, were kneeling beside the distressed horse, doing all they could to ease the pain.

Sean took a look at the mare and began calling orders. "I need warm water and plenty of blankets. And bring a cup of salt."

As everyone rushed to provide Sean what he needed, three riders approached from the west. Selina saw them first.

"Looks like Cole and Martha Santori. I think Cole's sister, Camilla, is with them."

Cole realized what was happening, dismounted, and dashed into the barn. "Colic?"

"Aye." Bram secured another blanket around the mare's abdomen.

"What can I do?"

"Help Sadie with the water. Remind her we need

salt."

Cole ran toward the house. Martha and Camilla watched from several feet away, boots rooted in place, gazes fixed on the sight before them.

Selina stroked the horse's face, applying warm compresses to comfort the mare. She talked to her in a soothing voice, working to keep her calm.

Cole rushed down the back stairs and into the barn, one hand holding a bucket of warm water, the other grasping a ten cup filled with salt.

"Where do you want these?"

"Next to Sean," Bram said.

Cole set them beside Sean before backing up to stand by his wife and sister.

"What's happening?" Camilla continued to stare, fascinated at what the MacLarens were doing.

Cole removed his hat, swiping an arm across his forehead. "The mare has a bad case of colic."

She took a small step forward. "Like in a child?"

"Yes, and no. Colic in horses can be fatal if not tended to right away. This mare is in tremendous pain." He blew out a breath. "I've seen more than one horse die from a bad case of colic."

Camilla watched as Sean worked, impressed by his calm demeanor and decisive actions. Sean's competence and sense of urgency to treat the ailing mare were apparent. She'd never witnessed such determination when an animal fell ill. In New York, most would put the creature out of its misery.

"Thane. Mix half the salt into a gallon of the warm water. Bram, we need to keep her as calm as possible. What I need to do next can be dangerous. I don't want the women close to the hindquarters."

Bram looked at his wife. "Selina, you and Sadie stay up at the mare's neck and head. Continue what you've been doing while Sean treats the mare."

Sadie joined Selina, rinsing the compresses in warm water before applying them across the mare's forehead. The horse whinnied but didn't move.

Sean opened his bag, retrieving a brass pump with a long nozzle attached to a plunger. Bram and Thane saw the instrument but restrained from commenting.

"We must get the mare to stand. It may take all of us. The procedure is safer for everyone if she's up." Sean looked around, noting the determination on each face. "Attach the halter and lead rope."

"This won't be easy." Bram got into position near Thane. He pointed to where he wanted Selina and Sadie.

"Ready?" Sean asked.

Everyone nodded.

"All right. One...two...three."

The mare fought their efforts for a moment before blowing air and standing.

Camilla put a hand over her mouth. "Oh, my..."

Beside her, Martha clasped a hand over her heart.

Bram secured the halter, holding the lead line as Thane wrapped a second line around the mare's neck.

Both men held her tight while Selina spoke in her ear while pressing warm towels against the mare's cheeks and forehead. Sadie kept the blankets around the horse's girth secure.

While the others secured and calmed the mare, Sean had been preparing the brass instrument, adding the water and salt mixture before spreading oil from his bag on the nozzle to ease entry into the mare. Holding the pump, Sean spoke gently to the horse as he administered the enema. The mare's legs churned at the discomfort, but Sean kept a steady hand on her flank.

"There now, easy girl," he murmured. "This will help, I promise."

Camilla watched, fascinated, as Sean worked to save the horse's life. His mix of calm and confidence captivated her. He ministered to an animal over five times his weight as if he were healing a child. Inserting the nozzle, he pumped in the solution.

Cole and Martha hung back. "Have you seen this type of procedure before?" she asked her husband.

"No, but I've heard about it. I hope it works."

Sean continued stroking the mare's hindquarters after removing the nozzle. She whinnied, though it was soft and shallow. Hearing a rumbling in the horse's abdomen, he stepped away, motioning Sadie to do the same. They moved a moment before the mare emptied the contents which had caused the impaction.

Sean's tense muscles relaxed as the horse passed

the blockage. Though still in distress, the mare was clearly doing better. The faces of those closest to the horse showed relief.

Camilla no longer saw the young veterinarian as just another rough westerner. Sean's skill and compassion revealed his refined nature despite outward appearances.

Sean continued talking and stroking the mare, her noticeable trembling eased. "You can ease the line around her neck, Thane. Bram, see if you can get her to walk around."

Camilla stepped forward, meeting Sean's gaze. "That was remarkable work. I can see why you graduated at the top of your class."

Though surprised by the compliment, Sean gave a slow nod. "Thank you, Miss Santori. Perhaps word will spread and people beyond my family will entrust me with their animals."

"They'd be fools not to," Camilla declared. "Why, if I had a ranch, you'd be the first one I'd call."

Her praise brought color to Sean's cheeks. He hadn't expected such high regard from this polished socialite.

Martha touched Camilla's shoulder. "Come along. Cole needs to get back to town. Incredible work, Sean."

"Thank you, Martha."

Camilla walked away, casting one last glance at the dedicated vet.

Chapter Five

Camilla stepped out of the wagon she shared with Martha, shielding her eyes from the bright morning sun. All around her, the air buzzed with activity as townsfolk swarmed over the skeleton of the new barn. Hammers pounded in a rhythmic beat as men and women worked side by side driving nails into the wooden beams.

A young couple approached, their cheeks flushed from exertion, eyes alight with enthusiasm. "Miss Santori!" The woman wiped her brow with the back of her hand. "So glad you could make it today."

Camilla smiled while rolling up the sleeves of her plain cotton dress. "I'm happy to help however I can."

The man grinned, handing her a hammer. "Well, there's plenty of work to go around."

With determination, Camilla set to work, the heavy hammer feeling foreign in her slender hands. She persevered, each swing driving the nail deeper into the wood. As she worked, her mind wandered back to the stiff parlors of New York, where her days had been occupied with frivolous gossip and tedious social calls. Here, she felt alive, immersed in the honest labor of common folks.

During a water break, Camilla engaged a family in

conversation, inquiring after their children and struggles after the long winter. She listened as the wife described their troubles, nodding with empathy. In turn, she shared stories of her own siblings and their lives in New York. Laughter flowed between them, and Camilla marveled at the wisdom and resilience of these modest ranchers.

Several times, she found herself searching the crowd of twenty or so people, hoping to find Sean among them. A surge of disappointment flowed through her when she didn't spot him.

Returning to work, her shoulders burned from the unaccustomed exertion. The pain didn't bother her. With each swing of the hammer, she felt a sense of accomplishment unlike anything in her previous life.

Later the same week, Camilla decided to attend an afternoon school meeting. Entering the schoolhouse, she stopped at the scent of wood polish familiar from her childhood days. Taking a seat among the parents and teachers, she smoothed her skirt, waiting for the meeting to begin.

Stan Petermann, owner of the general store, started by reviewing the actions of the last year. Their teacher, Rose Keenan, had accepted a position at the orphanage.

"Due to her decision, students from the town and

ranches had been taking their classes along with the orphans. The search for a new teacher was ongoing. As most of you know, we found a wonderful teacher to finish out the school year." He nodded toward a woman in the front row. "For those who don't know her, let me introduce Mrs. Dorinda Heaton. Please stand, Mrs. Heaton, so everyone can see you." Her face turned beet red as the crowd responded with enthusiastic clapping. Embarrassed, she sat back down when Stan continued.

"Now then, Mrs. Heaton has provided the town council with a list of concerns regarding students who are struggling with reading and sums..."

Camilla listened, her heart going out to those children, remembering her own difficulties learning letters and numbers.

"All right," Stan said. "I want to stress again, Rose Keenan has done a remarkable job under unusual circumstances. From what Miss Keenan and Mrs. Heaton have told us, it is quite common for a few students to struggle. What we need are ideas on how to help these children."

Camilla raised her hand. "I'm Miss Camilla Santori. Though I'm relatively new to Splendor, my suggestion would be to provide one-on-one tutoring for students who need it. This could be parents, or even those whose children are grown. I would be happy to volunteer."

Murmurs from the crowd moved another parent to disagree, while several supported Camilla's suggestion.

Other ideas were presented before the discussion moved to the upcoming Founder's Day events. Several people proposed ideas which had been used in the past.

Camilla spoke up again. "What about the children performing a play to highlight the town's history and the importance of education?"

Enthusiasm grew, with someone from the audience suggesting the children dress in costume, joyfully reciting their lines. Mrs. Heaton loved the idea and agreed to begin organizing rehearsals. She looked at Camilla.

"Miss Santori, would you have time to help?"

"I'd love to assist any way I can."

As the meeting concluded, she stepped outside into the afternoon sun, hopeful even these small actions could matter to Splendor's youth. Education had opened doors for her, and she wanted the same for these children.

Camilla decided to walk through Chinatown, visiting some shops, and perhaps enjoying a meal in one of the small restaurants. The rich aroma of spices and roasted duck floated onto the boardwalk. She paused to admire an elaborate robe in a store window, the silk embroidered with cranes and blossoms.

Without warning, a group of outlaws surrounded her. One stepped closer, bending to speak in her ear.

"Don't make a sound and everything will be all right."

Instead of showing fear as the outlaws expected,

she demanded answers. "What do you want?"

The man's hand moved to rest on the butt of his gun. "We've heard about you. The wealthy woman from back east. We've been waiting for the right moment."

She crossed her arms, glaring into his eyes. "For what?"

Hands on their holstered guns, the outlaws exchanged silent glances before another of the men spoke. "To take some of the wealth off your hands."

Anger and fear mingled inside Camilla, but she managed to keep her wits about her, searching for an opportunity to escape.

"Hand over yer valuables, missy, and you won't get hurt," growled the largest outlaw, his scruffy beard and yellowed teeth inches from her face.

Camilla's heart pounded, but she lifted her chin. "I have nothing of value to give you."

The outlaws pressed closer, hemming her in. Camilla cried out, the sound echoing down the street.

At the livery, Sean and Noah looked up at the cry, their conversation forgotten. Without hesitation, they rushed toward the commotion, instincts kicking in. Sean's hand moved to the six-shooter at his hip, ready to use it if needed. Noah did the same, his jaw set. They rounded the corner to see the outlaws surrounding Camilla.

"Step away from the lady," Sean commanded, his voice like steel.

The outlaws whirled toward him, caught off guard. Camilla's eyes met Sean's, flashing with equal parts terror and defiance. He felt a surge of protectiveness for this bold newcomer.

"You'll regret interrupting us," snarled the leader. "We'll be taking the lady and her valuables. Ain't nothing you can do about it."

Sean and Noah stood their ground. "I believe you're mistaken." Noah's calm manner and steely gaze bored into the outlaw's.

Sean's eyes glinted in controlled rage as his hand hovered near his holstered revolver.

"This is your last warning." Sean's voice was steady but carried an unmistakable threat. "Let the lady go and be on your way if you value your lives."

The outlaw leader didn't budge. "We'll take our chances."

In a flash, his hand dropped to his own gun. Sean and Noah were quicker, their revolvers up and firing before the outlaw could draw. The man cried out, clutching his shoulder as the bullet ripped into his flesh.

Chaos erupted. Gunshots echoed up and down the street at the exchange of fire. The outlaws scattered when Deputies Cash Coulter and Beau Davis ran forward, joining the gunfight.

Sean kept his eyes locked on Camilla, who'd taken cover in a store doorway. While Noah and the deputies provided cover, he moved in front of her, shielding her body with his own. She reached out, gripping his arm, her pulse racing.

"It's all right. I've got you." Sean fired twice more.

Spotting a break in the melee, he seized his chance. Keeping his body between Camilla and the flying bullets, he pulled her toward the Chinese market. Shoving open the door, they stumbled inside, hearts hammering.

"Back here, quick." He led her behind the counter at the same time the shopkeeper came out from behind curtains, waving his arms and shouting in Chinese.

Sean ignored him, pressing her down into a crouch to shelter her smaller frame with his larger one. They huddled together, scarcely daring to breathe as the sounds of gunfire continued outside.

She began to shake, adrenaline coursing through her veins. Sean wrapped an arm around her shoulders, offering what comfort he could.

"You're safe now."

She nodded, her body trembling, not quite believing his words as she clung to his offered strength, grateful for his steadying presence.

Sean held Camilla close as they hid behind the counter, the sounds of gunshots and shouts still ringing outside. Her breath came in short, panicked gasps as the terror of the attack sunk in.

"Shh, just keep breathing. I've got you." He rubbed her back gently.

After a few moments, the noises started to fade.

Sean peered cautiously over the counter. Seeing the street empty, he helped her to her feet.

"I think they're gone."

Camilla nodded, her legs unsteady.

He kept an arm around her as they slipped out the store's back entrance into an alley. They hurried along, pressed close to the buildings. Rounding a corner, Sean spotted a recessed doorway and pulled Camilla into its shadowed shelter.

They stood panting, adrenaline still coursing through their veins. Camilla leaned into Sean, taking comfort from his sturdy frame. His hand came up to steady her.

She blinked back tears, overwhelmed. Sean brushed a strand of hair from her face, his touch lingering. Somewhere nearby, a door banged shut, making her jump away. The spell broken, he grasped her hand.

"Come on, let's get you home."

Camilla nodded, allowing him to lead her down the alley. They moved cautiously, senses alert for any sign of the outlaws. Nearing the end of the alley, the sound of pounding hooves echoed down the adjacent street.

He pulled her into a recess between two buildings, pressing her back against the wall and shielding her body with his. Peering around the corner, he spotted a lone rider galloping toward them, six-shooter glinting in the sun.

The outlaw reined his horse to a stop just past their

hiding spot. Dismounting, he looked around, gun held ready. Camilla's breaths came quick and shallow against Sean's chest. He squeezed her hand, still gripping the revolver in his other hand.

Just as the outlaw reached the alley entrance, a shout rung out. "Hold it right there!"

Noah strode into view, revolver trained on the outlaw. Realizing he was outgunned, the outlaw froze. His eyes darted between Noah and the alley, calculating his odds. With a scowl, he turned and vaulted into the saddle, spurring his horse to a gallop.

Noah raised his revolver, sighting on the retreating man. A single shot pierced the early evening air. A moment later, the outlaw toppled off his horse to the ground.

Noah lowered his gun with a sigh of relief. He moved to check on Sean and Camilla. "You two all right?"

Sean nodded, exhaling a hard breath as the adrenaline drained away. Camilla sagged against him, the day's events catching up to her.

"We're okay, thanks to you. I think they hightailed it out of town for now." He tightened his arm around her.

Noah, never one to bask in praise, clasped his shoulder. "Let's get her home where it's safe."

Sean kept a protective arm around Camilla as they made their way to her house. Her slender frame trembled against him.

"Are you all right, Miss Santori?"

She took a deep breath to steady her nerves. "I'll be fine. Just...a bit rattled. Thank you for coming to my aid."

"I'm glad Noah and I were able to get to you in time." He paused a moment. "You kept your wits about you in the face of danger. Not every woman would have shown such courage, Miss Santori."

A hint of a smile tugged at her lips. "Please, call me Camilla."

"Camilla it is. And you're to call me Sean."

They walked in silence for a few moments. Despite their differences, Sean felt the beginning of a connection.

As they approached her house, he slowed. "Here we are, mi...Camilla. I'd rest up if I were you. Splendor may seem quiet, but it has its share of excitement."

Her eyes gleamed. "I'm starting to see that. Thank you again, Sean. I'm grateful for all you did."

He watched her disappear inside, intrigued by this newcomer stirring things up in their small town. With her wit and grit, he had a feeling Camilla Santori would be making quite an impression on Splendor.

Chapter Six

Camilla stood at her kitchen window, holding a cup of coffee while watching dawn creep over the distant ridges surrounding Splendor. A knot formed in her stomach as she recalled the kidnapping attempt just days before. She absently rubbed at the bruises on her arm, a stark reminder of the possible danger lurking even in this picturesque town.

Camilla was no fool. She knew the risks of being a wealthy, unmarried woman in the west. Still, she refused to be cowed by fear. Running back to the gilded cage of New York society was unthinkable. She'd come to Splendor to prove herself, to show she could handle adversity with courage and grace.

A knock at the door pulled Camilla from her reverie. Cole entered, his brow furrowed with concern. "You're up early," he said.

"Just watching the sunrise. It's beautiful here."

He nodded, his eyes grave. "Listen, Martha and I have been talking. After what happened, we're worried about you staying in Splendor alone. A single woman living by herself. It may not be safe."

Camilla bristled at the suggestion. "Now, Cole, we've discussed this. I know the risks, and I'm no shrinking violet. I can handle myself."

"No one's questioning your capability. The issue is you shouldn't have to constantly look over your shoulder. Martha and I only want what's best for you."

Camilla softened. She knew their concern came from a place of love. "I know. Please understand Splendor is my home now. Running back to New York won't solve anything."

She placed a hand on his shoulder. "I'm not going anywhere."

He studied her face, then nodded. "All right. Just promise you'll ask for help if you need it."

Camilla left home a few hours later with an idea in her head and a destination in mind. If the women of Splendor were to feel safe, real changes needed to happen.

She visited Gabe and Lena Evans' home first. As she walked up the porch steps, the front door opened and Lena appeared.

"Camilla. This is a pleasant surprise. Please, come in."

She stepped into the cozy living room where Gabe sat reading the local newspaper. He set it down and stood to greet her.

"Good to see you," Gabe said. "Sit down and tell us what brings you out this way."

"I wanted to discuss an idea with both of you." Camilla lowered herself onto a big chair sized more for a man than a woman. She outlined her thoughts. "A town meeting is needed to address safety concerns and find solutions."

Lena's face grew serious. "You're right, something must be done. The women deserve to feel safe."

"A meeting's a good thought. Folks need a chance to voice their worries and collaborate," Gabe said.

"Will you two help spread the word?" Camilla asked. "Your support will go a long way."

"Of course. Just say when," Lena answered.

"How about day after tomorrow? The sooner the better."

"I'll alert my deputies, too," Gabe assured her.

They discussed a time for the meeting, which would be held at the community building.

Camilla's spirits lifted at their readiness to help. She bid them goodbye, filled with optimism.

Her next stop was the home of Nick and Suzanne Barnett. She was surprised to see Suzanne open the door. Most days, you could find her at the boardinghouse restaurant.

"Come in. May I get you coffee or tea?"

Soon, Camilla was seated with a cup of hot coffee and one of Suzanne's famous blueberry muffins. As Nick joined them, she shared her idea for the town meeting.

He listened, brow furrowed. "You're right,

something must be done. The women here shouldn't have to live in fear."

Suzanne nodded. "A meeting's a fine notion. We'll spread the word to folks at the boardinghouse."

Camilla smiled, buoyed by their support. With the community behind her, real progress could be made.

The day of the town meeting arrived, and the community hall was filled to overflowing. Camilla stood at the front, heartened to see so many faces, both men and women, gathered to address the issue of women's safety.

She cleared her throat, suddenly nervous. The crowd quieted and all eyes turned to her. Drawing a deep breath, she began.

"Thank you for coming today. As you know, the recent attack has many of Splendor's women concerned for their safety." Murmurs of assent rippled through the crowd.

"It's time we take action to protect ourselves and look out for one another." More sounds of agreement followed. Camilla went on to outline potential ideas, opening the discussion up to the crowd.

Many voiced their thoughts and concerns. The room buzzed with vigorous debate about possible solutions. After passionate discussion, one idea rose to the top—teaching women how to shoot.

Just then, Gabe stood up and called for attention. "If it's training you ladies want, my deputies and I would be pleased to provide it."

Sean rose as well. "I'll volunteer my time, too. My shooting skills are a bit rusty, but I'm happy to share what I know."

A murmur of excitement went through the crowd. The first training session was slated for the following week. When the meeting adjourned, some of the women continued to chat about this new chapter ahead, excitement in their voices. Optimism filled the room.

The week passed swiftly. A large group of Splendor's women gathered in a field outside the south end of town. Many more than expected. Gabe, Sean, and three deputies were there to provide instruction. Camilla felt a quiver of anticipation as she joined the others.

Sean stepped forward holding a six-shooter. "All right, ladies, let's get started. This is how you load a Colt revolver..."

The session passed in a blur of activity. With Gabe and the deputies backing him up, Sean took his time guiding them through loading, aiming, and firing the six-shooter. Afterward, Deputy Beth Evans demonstrated proper shotgun technique.

Though new and strange at first, Camilla grew more confident with each round fired. From the proud smiles around her, she could tell the other women felt the same.

When Gabe called for a break in the training, talk turned to scheduling the next one. The women were clearly hungry to hone their newfound skills. As Camilla looked around at the group, she was filled with hope. The women of Splendor were taking fate into their own hands.

Sean watched Camilla as she practiced loading and firing the revolver. Her eyes shone with determination, her stance exuded strength.

He felt a surge of admiration for this woman. Her courage and resilience stirred something within him he didn't expect. She was unlike any woman he'd known.

As Camilla laughed and talked with the other ladies, Sean grappled with his growing feelings. He'd always thought her too refined and stubborn. Seeing her in this light changed his perspective. She'd proven herself to be capable and resourceful.

Could he have misjudged her? The wall he'd built between them now seemed insignificant. Try as he might, he couldn't tear his gaze away as she handled both the revolver and shotgun with unexpected confidence.

All around him, the women chatted about their new skills. An unforeseen bond had developed between them. For the first time, these ladies felt they had skills to protect themselves.

"We have to do this again," said May Covington, the wife of Deputy Caleb Covington. "My husband taught me to use a shotgun, but learning with other women is so much more fun."

"Oh, yes. This makes me want to learn more," exclaimed Carrie MacKenzie, a nurse at the clinic.

Lena clapped her hands to get everyone's attention. "Ladies, that was marvelous. I feel safer already."

Murmurs of agreement rippled through the crowd, the women vocal in their appreciation.

"We should do this every week." Olivia McCord, Doctor Clay McCord's wife, couldn't keep the smile off her face.

After a brief discussion with Gabe, Camilla stepped forward. "I'm so glad this first session was a success. We'll plan to meet again next Thursday for more practice. The more we train together, the better prepared we'll be."

The women nodded, faces flushed with exhilaration. As they parted ways, hugs and words of encouragement were exchanged. A feeling of unity filled the air.

From the edge of the crowd, Sean watched Camilla bask in the glow of accomplishment. She'd achieved something meaningful here today. Though they clashed at times, he respected her determination to create change.

Sean walked back to his veterinary office, lost in thought. The sight of Camilla handling a shotgun with such poise and precision had left an impression. He couldn't deny she had a boldness and resilience that challenged his preconceived notions.

With a sigh, he entered his office, emotions churning. The walls between them had narrowed, but he had no intention of letting them crumble.

When he saw her again, he'd be cordial but distant, as always. She was a neighbor in need of his protection and nothing more. The walls between them must remain standing, for both their sakes.

Sean buried himself in his work over the next few days, emerging from his office for meals and the occasional errand around town. He avoided the restaurants and anywhere else he might run into Camilla, not trusting himself to maintain an emotional distance if they spoke.

At night, he lay awake replaying their interactions, cursing himself for being so affected by her. Why couldn't he view her with the same detached concern he felt toward other women? What was it about her that slipped through the cracks in his armor?

Try as he might, he couldn't stop wondering about Camilla's past and what had brought her out west alone. Perhaps they weren't so unalike after all. But it was a dangerous line of thinking, one he must not indulge.

When the day of the next training session arrived,

Sean considered staying away. Yet his conscience wouldn't allow it. These women were relying on the men to teach them how to protect themselves. Avoiding his duties would be irresponsible.

He walked to the field where makeshift targets had been set up. A crowd of women gathered, abuzz with excitement. Gabe was already there, handing out shotguns to each eager pupil.

Sean scanned the faces until his eyes fell on Camilla. She caught his gaze for a moment before looking away. Was that a hint of pink in her cheeks? No, surely it was just the exertion of hauling the heavy gun.

"Glad you could join us, Doc." Gabe waved Sean over.

Sean tipped his hat in greeting. Seeing the number of women who'd returned for a second lesson made him smile.

Gabe addressed the group. "All right, ladies, let's review what we learned last time."

As the lesson commenced, Sean hung back, observing. Camilla stood erect, her focus intent as she aimed and fired at the target. The recoil didn't bother her anymore. Her confidence continued to increase with each shot.

In only a short time, she'd transformed from a refined socialite into a gritty frontierswoman. Though hesitant at first, she now embraced this new way of life.

When the shooting ended, the women gathered to

chat and laugh. Camilla's eyes sparkled, her cheeks flushed pink beneath a light sheen of sweat and dirt.

Before he could stop himself, he was walking toward her. She noticed his approach, her expression shifting to one of uncertainty. He opened his mouth, unsure what he planned to say.

"That was some fine shooting, Camilla."

She smiled tentatively. "Thank you. There's still a lot to learn."

They stood in awkward silence for a moment. He rubbed the back of his neck, chastising himself for seeking her out on impulse.

Camilla spoke first. "Well, I should be going. Thank you again for doing this. It means a great deal."

Sean tipped his hat. "Of course. Enjoy your day."

As she walked away, he let out a heavy sigh. These feelings were foolish. Pursuing them would only lead to heartache. Turning toward town, he walked home, thoughts of Camilla still lingering against his will.

Chapter Seven

Dust kicked up under the hooves of Luke Pelletier's chestnut stallion as he galloped toward Splendor, urgency etched onto his features like the furrows of a plowed field. His mind filled with images of what he'd seen—the reason Bull had awakened him and Dax so early.

The morning sun had barely crested the horizon when Bull Mason, one of the ranch's two foremen, pounded on the front door of Redemption's Edge Ranch. It only took a look at his face to know something serious was wrong

As he rode toward town, Luke recalled what he and Dax had seen not twenty minutes earlier.

Dax Pelletier, hands on hips, Luke beside him, stared down at the carcass of a steer. Another dead animal lay less than twenty feet away. He'd looked at Bull.

"What do you think happened to them?" Dax's voice carried over the pasture, roughened by both concern and command. As a former battlefield general in the Southern Army, he knew how to assert authority.

"Can't say for sure, boss." Bull scratched his short beard. "I've never seen this before. There are at least ten more head showing the same symptoms."

The Pelletier brothers had stood beside their foreman, surveying the ailing herd. Several cattle lay prone, too weak to stand, while others huddled listlessly. The two carcasses sprawled on the ground were an ominous warning of what might come should they fail to act swiftly.

"Get to town, Luke. Fetch Sean MacLaren," Dax ordered, his gaze never leaving the sickly beasts. "We need him yesterday."

Luke offered a curt nod before spurring his horse into a thunderous sprint, the urgency of the situation fueling his ride.

In Splendor, Sean MacLaren leaned against the wooden frame of his modest veterinary clinic, a cup of coffee in his hand, squinting at the approaching rider. The clatter of hooves broke the stillness of the morning, and soon enough, Luke reined up. Tossing out the rest of his coffee, Sean met him at the edge of the steps.

"What is it?"

"It's bad. Two cattle are dead and at least ten more ailing. We have no idea what's happening. We need you out there."

Sean motioned him inside, his calm demeanor belying the quickening of his own pulse. "Tell me what you saw as I pack my bag, then we'll ride back to your ranch."

As Luke described the lethargic cattle with coughs

and abscesses, Sean's expression grew grave. From those few symptoms, he had an idea what was affecting the cattle. He also knew the Pelletier ranch was at risk if this illness spread further.

"Have you seen anything like this before?" Luke hovered in the doorway, his eyes betraying the fear gripping his heart.

"I can't say without seeing them. Bovine ailments come in many shades, some deadlier than others." Sean secured the strap on his bag. His mind raced through the possible diseases, preparing himself for the worst, even as he hoped for something benign.

"My horse is at the livery."

Luke mounted his horse, holding out a hand to help Sean climb on behind him. He kicked his horse into a gallop, rushing through town before reining up at the livery. Ten minutes later, they were on their way.

As they rode, the weight of the rancher's predicament hung heavy in the air, each man grappling with the potential devastation looming over the Pelletier legacy.

A sense of foreboding accompanied them as the two reached the pasture and dismounted. Bull, the lines on his face etched deeper by concern, stood sentinel over the ailing herd.

Dax shook Sean's hand. "Thanks for coming. We have a real problem."

"Doc," Bull greeted with a curt nod.

Sean's gaze roamed over the cattle, taking in each

hacking cough, the listless droop of their heads, and the unsightly lumps marring their hides. He noted the abscesses with a clinical detachment necessary to perform his duties, yet his heart clenched for each labored breath he witnessed.

"They've been dropping weight the last few days. I should've realized we had something serious going on." Bull's voice rumbled with frustration.

"Show me the carcasses." Sean masked his growing alarm with a calm he didn't quite feel.

They approached the two lifeless forms lying a respectful distance away. Flies buzzed in a macabre dance of death, and the stench of decay lay thick in the air. Sean knelt beside the nearest one, his hands steady as he pulled out his knife and made the first incision. The others watched in silence, the tension between them taut enough to strum.

"Lord have mercy," Bull muttered under his breath.

As Sean peeled back the layers of skin and muscle, his suspicions solidified into a dreadful certainty. Lesions littered the lungs, and the lymph nodes were swollen and deformed—a testament to the ravages of bovine tuberculosis.

"Sean?" Luke's voice cracked the stillness, carrying with it the weight of their livelihood, their heritage.

"Give me a moment," Sean said, his tone even but firm. He needed time to gather his thoughts, to plan their next steps. This wasn't just a matter of medicine.

It could be a battle for the future of Redemption's Edge.

Rising to his feet, Sean wiped his blade clean. "We've got a serious problem on our hands. We need to act swiftly."

He met their gazes, seeing the reflection of his own resolve mirrored in their eyes. They understood the stakes.

"Isolate them." Sean's voice carried the weight of authority born from knowledge and a grim experience. "Every head that coughs, looks weary, or is dropping in weight needs to be separated from the herd. And those with lumps or abscesses—" He paused, searching the faces of Dax, Luke, and Bull, each one etched with the gravity of the situation. "Cull them. It's the only way to contain it."

Dax's jaw tightened, the muscles ticking in frustration. "Cull them? That's a heavy loss, Sean. Are you certain?"

"Dead certain. It's bovine tuberculosis. If we don't act now, you might not have a herd left to worry over."

Luke swore under his breath, kicking at the dirt. "We can't afford this, not now." His hand moved reflexively to his hip, seeking reassurance in the worn handle of his revolver.

"Better to lose some than all." Bull's eyes creased with concern. "You know the doc's right, Luke. We do what we must."

"All right." Dax gave a sharp nod. "We'll do what

you say, Sean. You got any notion how to treat this scourge?"

"None that I know of, but I'll find out. I'm heading back to town to hit the books. There's got to be something."

"Appreciate it." Luke clasped a hand on Sean's shoulder. "If anyone can figure a way out of this mess, it's you."

Sean nodded, already mentally compiling a list of veterinary texts and journals he'd need to scour. He mounted his horse with a grace that spoke of a life spent as much in the saddle as in the study of medicine. The animal shifted beneath him, sensing the urgency of their return journey.

"Keep me posted," Dax called out as Sean urged his horse toward town.

"Will do!"

Once in town, Sean's boots echoed on the wood floor of his home. He tossed his hat and coat on a chair before walking to the room which served as his clinic, office, and library. The door creaked open when he entered.

Time passed as Sean pored over the medical volumes, his fingers tracing lines of text while his mind raced for solutions. Diagrams, case studies, and the dry language of scientific inquiry filled the pages.

"Come on, there's got to be something," he muttered to himself, the frustration evident in his furrowed brow.

The afternoon sun began its downward descent, casting long shadows through the window panes as Sean finally pushed away the books and stood. His mind buzzed with half-formed ideas.

Sean's boots clipped along the boardwalk as he walked, his mind wrestling with the grim task ahead. Though his shoulders tensed against it, the weight of the cattle crisis bore down on him. As he passed the general store, the bell above the door jingled. Camilla stepped into the afternoon glare.

"Hello, Sean."

"Camilla." He touched the brim of his hat.

"I was on my way to your house to ask if you'll be at the training session this week."

"Training will have to wait. The Pelletier herd's got sick cattle. I've been out there. It looks like bovine tuberculosis."

"Mercy." Her hand came to rest at the base of her throat. "I've heard of it. From the little I know, that's dire news for the Pelletiers. The whole town, really."

"Spread of the disease could ruin not just one ranch, but all those around Splendor." He glanced away for a moment, toward the north where the Pelletier lands lay. "We may need to cull much of the herd to contain it."

Camilla's brow furrowed, her usual air of authority

giving way to concern. "Is there anything I can do?" The question hung between them, surprising even her with its earnestness.

"Help?" Sean echoed, skepticism lacing his tone, a stark contrast to her selfless proposal.

"It's a sincere offer. If I can be of use in saving those animals, then it's work worth doing."

Sean studied her for a long moment, the fine lines of her face telling stories of resolve he'd not taken the time to read before. "All right, Camilla. Your help would be welcome."

"Thank you. I'm ready to learn, and to do whatever it takes."

Sean strode toward the Splendor clinic the following morning, his mind a maelstrom of worry and resolve. The gravity of what he had to share weighed on him like saddlebags filled with lead.

"Drake, Clay," Sean called out as he entered the clinic. The two doctors came down the stairs to stand a few feet from him. Neither had a chance to greet him.

"There's a notion bovine tuberculosis could jump to humans. I need your thoughts."

Drake Ralston set aside the bandage he was rolling, his eyes meeting Sean's with an intensity born of his military past. He and Clay had heard about the outbreak at the Pelletier ranch. "That's a grim prospect, Sean. What makes you suspect it?"

"Symptoms and lesions in the cattle are textbook cases." Sean unwrapped the cloth around a jar that held a grim sample. "I took these from the Pelletiers' stock. We need to know if we're dealing with more than just livestock at risk."

Clay McCord leaned over the jar, peering intently at the contents. His surgeon's hands, steady even after years away from the battlefield, betrayed no tremor of concern. "We'll have to look at this under magnification. Follow me."

Drake's gaze flickered with understanding as he lifted the jar, careful as one might handle a stick of dynamite. "Sean, if this is what you fear, it could change everything for Splendor."

"Which is why we must tread carefully. Not only for the ranchers, but for every soul here."

"Agreed." Drake nodded. "Let's see where science leads us."

Camilla stepped through the narrow door of the medicinal herb shop in Chinatown, a mingling scent of ginseng and dried chrysanthemums enveloped her. The shelves were lined with jars and bundles of herbs, their labels inscribed with characters she couldn't decipher. The shopkeeper, a man of advanced years with a face as lined as an old map, looked up from his task of grinding herbs.

"May I assist you?" he asked in heavily accented English, peering at her over his spectacles.

Camilla cleared her throat. "I'm seeking advice on an illness affecting cattle—bovine tuberculosis. Is there... might there be a remedy you know of?"

The shopkeeper stroked his thin beard, considering her with sharp eyes. "A serious ailment. But perhaps not without hope. Come."

He led her to a shelf where small packets of dried leaves lay neatly stacked. "This is eucalyptus. It does much to ease coughs, could help afflicted cattle breathe. And here." He offered another packet. "Astragalus. For vigor. It strengthens immune response."

The man moved along the shelves before stopping to pick up another pouch. "This is called echinacea. In China, it is used on sick animals to help them recover."

He walked several feet to the end of the aisle. "This is fenugreek for coughs and lung afflictions." A smile crept across his face, making him appear years younger. "I have a special mix of herbs. You mix it into paste and put on lesions. I have seen it work on animals."

Camilla studied the packets, knowing it wouldn't be enough to stop the spread of the disease. "Do you have more of these?"

"Ah, yes. There are large sacks of herbs in the back."

"Thank you, Mr..."

"Chen."

"Thank you, Mr. Chen. These may be exactly what we need."

She purchased a generous supply of each, nodding respectfully to Mr. Chen. Stepping back into the sunlight, her steps quickened as she hurried to find Sean.

She didn't have to go far. He stood on the boardwalk, talking with Sheriff Evans. Their conversation was cut short by the sound of her footsteps. Camilla stopped next to them.

"We'll talk again, Sean." Gabe nodded at Camilla before walking toward the jail.

"I may have found something." She held up the packets from the herb shop.

"From Chinatown?" Sean asked, a flicker of interest crossing his features.

Camilla nodded, explaining the properties of each large bag of herbs. "It's worth trying, don't you think?"

Chapter Eight

Sean looked between the bags and Camilla. "We have nothing else to offer the Pelletiers. Let's go to my clinic so you can explain everything about administering the herbs. If what you were told makes sense, we'll prepare what we need for the cattle."

Within a few minutes, they were standing at a counter in the area Sean used for his clinic. Camilla explained what Mr. Chen had told her, pointing to different bags.

"He wouldn't tell me what he used in the poultice mixture, but he believed it might be successful for treating the lesions." She went on to explain how to administer the herbs to the sick animals.

Sean listened with interest, writing down his thoughts in a journal. When she finished, he set the journal aside.

"We'll prepare the herb mixture into pastes to spread over the exterior lesions. The echinacea and astralagus will be mixed into their feed. The fenugreek is a little more difficult. I believe the best approach would be to burn it so the cattle may inhale the herb. I'll talk with the Pelletiers and Bull about other options. Did Mr. Chen stock garlic?"

"He didn't mention it, but he has shelves filled with products."

"I'm assuming you want to ride out with me?" Sean asked.

Her back stiffened. "Of course."

He held up a hand, stifling a chuckle. "I'll get a wagon from Noah while you return to Chen's shop. Buy any garlic he has and meet me at the livery."

They were on the trail to the Pelletier ranch within thirty minutes, both hoping for a breakthrough with the herbs. Sean had learned much during his time at the university. What he learned from local women around Edinburgh was a different educational experience.

The use of herbs and other native plants to treat people and animals had been practiced for centuries, the knowledge passed from one generation to the next. In cases where scientific medicine produced no results, there could still be hope in the old traditions.

Sean drove the wagon to the scene of the affected cattle, finding Dax, Luke, Bull, and several other ranch hands busy checking each animal and sorting them into groups. Clean animals were moved to another pasture, while those showing symptoms were kept not far from the culled animals.

The Pelletiers and Bull held rifles, their blank

stares indicating the difficulty of their actions. Stopping the wagon close to them, Sean helped Camilla down.

"We may have another option for the sick cattle. If you're willing to try it."

Dax shoved his hat from his forehead. "We'll do whatever we can to save them, Sean."

"Good." He went on to explain what Camilla had learned from Mr. Chen, surprised all three men knew of the man's small shop. Finishing, he waited for a response.

Dax set his rifle aside. "Tell us what to do."

As they worked, the sun dipped lower, casting an orange glow over the desperate scene. Camilla couldn't help but notice the lines of worry etched deep on each man's face. Yet there was also determination in each set of eyes. When her gaze landed on Sean, she couldn't help feeling a rush of kinship. They worked together as if born to this kind of collaboration.

"Camilla?"

She startled, embarrassed at him catching her staring. "Yes?"

Sean closed the distance between them in a few easy steps. "This...collaboration. It's unexpected but appreciated."

Odd how she'd been thinking the same. "We have a common cause. I hope what we're doing makes an impact on the herd."

"Indeed." Sean offered a wry smile.

They finished treating the first of the sick cattle, watching for any sign of improvement or deterioration. The animals' eyes met theirs, a silent plea for relief tightened Camilla's chest.

As dusk settled over the ranch, Sean and Camilla stood side by side, two unlikely allies bound together by the plight of Splendor and the fragile thread of hope they now held between them.

With the last light fading, Sean cast a long look toward the horizon. He turned toward the other men. "We'll return at dawn. With luck, our efforts will bear fruit."

"Whatever happens, Sean, we appreciate your efforts," Dax said. "Yours, too, Camilla."

They boarded the wagon, tired yet hopeful the treatments worked. For now, all they could do was wait, ignoring the bitter taste of uncertainty lingering in the air.

The air in Sean's office was heavy with the lingering scent of dried herbs. Two oil lamps flickered across his face as he pored over the texts splayed before him, his eyes scanning for any mention of bovine tuberculosis treatments he may have missed earlier.

This search focused on treatments for humans who may have contracted the disease from exposure to the sick animals.

"Any luck?" Camilla Santori's voice cut through the silence, her slender form perched on the chair across the desk from Sean.

They'd eaten a late dinner at McCall's before returning to his office. She'd been surprised when he'd invited her to come along, help him go through the journals and books.

"Perhaps," Sean murmured without looking up. "Here." He pointed to a passage in an old leather-bound journal. "Certain herbs have been used to boost immunity and combat similar infections in people." He looked up. "I need to show this to Drake and Clay. Neither had any information of the disease passing to humans. The sample didn't prove anything. If it does happen here, they'll need to consider using the same methods we're utilizing at the ranch."

"Mr. Chen also mentioned licorice root, though I didn't buy any. It has anti-inflammatory properties."

"Good to know."

"At least this is better than standing by while those ranchers lose everything." Camilla's voice was laced with a hard edge born of witnessing too much suffering. Including her father's deterioration before he passed.

"Agreed. I want to administer a second round of herbs at first light. The same in the late afternoon, monitoring each animal for any sign of improvement or decline."

"If this doesn't work, we may be facing the end of

the Pelletier ranch as we know it." The gravity in her voice settled over them like a shroud.

"Let's focus on the best possible outcome, shall we?" Sean reached for her hand in a rare gesture of camaraderie. Their fingers touched briefly, before she abruptly stood.

"I should go home before it's completely dark. I'll return at dawn." Camilla tucked her hand in a pocket, mustering a semblance of her usual poise. Even this effort didn't erase the tingle where they'd touched.

He stood to open the door. "I'll walk you home."

"Don't be silly. I can see the side of my house from here."

"If you're sure." Sean watched her until she reached the front door, feeling a mix of admiration and anxiety. He felt the loss of her presence, his chest tightening as if in distress.

Dawn's light was already casting long shadows across the Pelletier ranch when Sean and Camilla arrived. The horses pulling the wagon kicked up clouds of dust suspended in the crisp morning air. They jumped to the ground with a sense of urgency, ready to get the second round of treatment underway.

"Morning, Sean. Camilla." Dax touched his hat, his usual smile tinged with worry.

"You're here early," Sean responded.

Luke looked toward the eastern horizon. "We never left. The three of us, plus several of our ranch hands, stayed here."

"I'm not surprised." Sean removed the bags of herbs from the wagon.

"Let's hope this works." Luke joined his brother, eyes fixed on the suffering cattle.

Together, with Bull Mason's assistance, they administered the second treatment. Sean carefully mixed some of the Chinatown herbs into a paste.

Camilla took the lead with a gentle touch, whispering soothing words to one of the larger animals. "Easy now." She stroked its neck before applying the herbal concoction to small lesions on the animal's flank.

"Never figured you for the cattle type, Miss Santori," Bull remarked, a hint of respect in his voice.

"Nor I." Camilla continued to smooth the paste over what appeared to be a rash on the animal's hide.

As the sun climbed higher, everyone worked without pause, moving from one ailing creature to the next. Sweat beaded on their brows, their hands staining with the green and brown hues of the herbal mixture.

When finished with the paste, they tossed herbs on the feed. As the infected herd ate, the men and Camilla kept watch for any changes, already knowing improvement would be a slow process.

At noon, Rachel and Ginny Pelletier drove a wagon

out with food and water. As everyone ate, Dax described how the men had checked the other herds, finding no trace of the disease.

"Does that mean if we can get the tuberculosis under control here, it won't spread?" Luke asked.

"It's possible," Sean answered. "Have you combined any of the cattle from the infected herd with other animals?"

"No," Bull said right away. "Each herd has been quarantined separately."

"Then I'd say you have an excellent chance of controlling the spread. I'm happy to check any of the herds while I'm here."

When Sean and Bull returned from examining the other herds, both felt a surge of solid hope. They arrived just as the others were applying the late afternoon applications. The two didn't hesitate before helping out, sharing what they'd found on their trip around the ranch.

Finishing, the group stepped away, tired but encouraged. If only they could spot improvement in at least one infected animal.

"Look there, Sean." Camilla pointed at a steer they'd treated three times. The beast, once lethargic and coughing, now stood more upright, nosing curiously at the hay on the ground.

"Could it be possible?" Sean squinted against the sunlight to get a better look. He approached the steer, placing a hand on its neck and feeling for swollen lymph nodes. "The swelling... it's gone down."

"Does this mean..." Camilla's voice trailed off.

"It's too early to say for sure," Sean cautioned, though a faint smile threatened to break through his professional veneer. "But it's a positive sign."

"Would you look at that." Dax joined them, a mixture of disbelief and optimism in his voice. "You may have saved us, Doctor MacLaren."

"Let's not count our blessings just yet." Sean looked over the steer once more before stepping away. "We'll need to monitor them closely over the next few days."

Dax nodded. "Of course. But seeing how the steer improved is something I didn't expect to witness so soon."

"Neither did I." Sean allowed himself a moment to bask in the tentative victory.

As the group dispersed, continuing their respective tasks with renewed vigor, Sean caught Camilla's attention. They shared an unspoken understanding, a partnership forged under the most trying of circumstances.

As everyone packed up the herbs in the back of the wagon, a solitary figure remained near the treated cattle. In the fading light, Sean allowed himself to believe maybe, just maybe, they'd turned the tide against the silent enemy threatening to claim the lifeblood of Redemption's Edge.

The following morning, Camilla knelt beside another listless animal, her skirts bunched without care for propriety, her fingers deft as she followed Sean's instructions.

"This one's breathing easier than yesterday," she called over her shoulder.

"Good." Sean straightened, wiping his brow with the back of his forearm. "We'll need every victory we can muster."

"Do you think the herbs from Chinatown are truly the answer?" Bull's weathered face was hard to read, but his eyes betrayed guarded optimism.

"Medicine is part trial, part error, Bull." Sean locked eyes with the foreman. "All we can do now is continue administering the herbs, wait, and watch."

"Waiting has never been my strong suit," Bull grumbled, but there was no heat in his words.

"Nor mine." Camilla rose to her feet, strength radiating from her despite the grime and fatigue that clung to her frame. "But if this works..."

"Then we've done more than most would have," Sean finished for her.

"Still, hard to believe a lady like yourself would know a thing about cattle sickness," Dax mused, watching Camilla with an unreadable expression.

"Perhaps you'll find most ladies can be full of surprises," Camilla shot back, her tone playful, yet edged with steel.

"I've been learning that every day since arriving in Splendor all those years ago," Dax conceded with a wry smile.

"Indeed." Sean chuckled. Pausing, he looked out over the herd. "There's a chance we might just beat this blight."

"From your lips to God's ears," Dax said quietly, his spirits rising for the first time in days.

Chapter Nine

Sean rode to the sprawling Pelletier ranch the following morning, eager to examine the cattle he'd treated. As he approached the sight where the infected cattle had been isolated, Luke and Dax Pelletier walked over to greet him, broad smiles on their weathered faces.

"Morning, Doc." Luke extended his hand as Sean dismounted. "We've been keeping a close watch on the herd since yesterday. Those treatments of yours appear to be working."

Sean relaxed at the news. "I'm glad the herbs were effective."

He felt a stab of regret Camilla couldn't have been able to join him for the praise. Her volunteer commitment at the orphanage took precedence today.

Dax clasped Sean on the shoulder. "We haven't lost a single head of cattle since yesterday. You must have some kind of magic in those potions of yours."

"Not mine. They belong to Mr. Chin in Chinatown."

"However it came about, the cattle are improving," Dax added as the men joined Bull to inspect the herd.

Sean noticed the improvement right away. Dax turned to him.

"We appreciate all you've done. You saved this

herd, and in turn, saved our ranch. We won't forget it."

"I'd suggest we continue the treatment for at least two more days. Do you feel comfortable administering the herbs without me here?"

"No problem, Doc." Bull pointed to a stack of half-full bags. "We've already completed the morning treatment. There's enough for three more days. Will that do?"

"Should be fine. I'll ride out day after tomorrow to make a final check. I'd be happy to examine the other herds to confirm the infection didn't spread."

"We'd appreciate it," Dax said. "Luke and I will go with you."

Four hours later, Sean rode back to Splendor, touched by the Pelletiers' sincere gratitude for his efforts. Approaching town, a dust cloud in the distance signaled an approaching rider. He reined to a stop when Noah Brandt slowed next to him, face etched with concern.

"Afternoon, Noah. What brings you out this way?"

Dismounting, Noah's expression was grim. "I've got troubling news, Sean. Word in town is someone's been spreading rumors, questioning your skills as a veterinarian. Somebody claims you came to his ranch and your treatment killed his stallion."

Sean's eyes widened in shock. "That's outrageous. I've done no such thing. I haven't treated a stallion at anyone's ranch, except for the ones at my cousins' place."

Noah nodded. "I didn't think the claims could be

true. But folks are starting to whisper, and I thought you should know before you got back to town."

"Appreciate it, Noah."

Sean's thoughts raced, confusion and anger swirling within him. Who would spread such condemning lies? And to what end? He needed to find the source of these rumors and set the record straight. His reputation and practice depended on it.

Sean's jaw tightened as he turned to Noah. "I have to stop these unfounded accusations. My skills are sound, and I won't let anyone threaten my practice with false rumors."

"I'll do what I can to help you get to the bottom of this."

They rode back to town, his mind working to identify potential suspects. As they hitched their horses outside the Dixie saloon, Noah spoke up.

"I believe the best way to identify the person is to ask outright."

Sean nodded. "Discreetly."

Noah offered a wry grin.

They entered the saloon, the air thick with tobacco smoke and an odd silence. Noah didn't expect too many people to be inside this early in the afternoon. He hoped the slim number of men might make it easier to obtain a name. Moving to the bar, they ordered whiskey and began subtly eavesdropping on conversations around them.

After some time, Noah leaned in. "I only recognize

a couple of the men. One's a farmer who delivers his crop to the general store. The other owns the bakery and meat market. He always comes in after his wife brings in more of her baked goods at noon. She takes over so he can eat lunch. They're at the same table to our right. The farmer, he's wearing the stained dark gray hat, sure seems riled up about something. I've heard him going on about incompetent outsiders before." Noah sipped his whiskey. "It's all right for him to move here, but no one else."

Sean's eyes narrowed, watching the farmer's mouth twist into a grimace. "He does seem perturbed about something. I don't believe I've ever seen him before. Can't imagine why he'd spread rumors about me."

"Only one way to find out." Noah tilted his head toward the doors. "I'll talk to him when he leaves. Stay out of sight. He might not talk if he sees you."

An hour passed before the farmer stepped onto the boardwalk. Removing his hat, the man looked around, surprised when Noah joined him.

"Afternoon, Roy. Got a minute?"

Roy swayed, squinting at him. "What do you want, Brandt?"

"Well now, I heard some troubling talk about the new veterinarian in town. You wouldn't know anything about the rumors, would you?"

Roy tipped his head back on a burst of laughter. "You talking about the newcomer?"

"Sean MacLaren."

The farmer swayed again, his eyes a watery red. "Might know something."

"Did you start the rumors?"

"No, I ain't the one to start them." Roy reached out to brace himself against a post. "Doesn't mean I don't believe them. Figured everyone in town should know about the incompetent con."

"Con? How do you figure?"

"Anyone pretending to be one of those veter...veterians...well, animal doc...he must be lying. There's no such a thing." He flashed Noah a yellow-toothed grin.

"You've never met a veterinarian before?"

"Like I said. There's no such thing. Means the man's a fraud." Roy lifted a booted foot to step onto the dirt street, stopping when Noah grabbed his arm.

"Care to explain why you're spreading lies about his work instead of confronting the doc?" Noah asked.

Roy's face flushed. "Ain't no lies. He's a fraud and a fool. My friend told me MacLaren treated his prize stallion. The animal died right after."

"Who's your friend?"

"I ain't gonna say."

"Well then, how about we have a talk with Sheriff Evans. You can talk to him." Noah figured his longtime friend, Gabe, couldn't do anything. Still, it was worth getting a reaction from Roy.

"I don't know about talking to the law. I gotta get

back to my place.”

Noah took his arm, propelling him toward the street and the jail.

“Wait up now.” Roy dragged his boot heels into the dirt. “Let go and I’ll tell ya.”

Letting go, Noah crossed his arms and waited.

“Mick.”

“Mick who?”

“All I know is Mick.”

“Where can I find him?”

Scratching the back of his neck, Roy shook his head. “Can’t say as I know.” After a breath, he nodded. “I think he’s the one staying at the boardinghouse. Yep, that’s him.”

Noah studied him before nodding. “You need help getting home?”

“Nah. I do this all the time.”

He watched as Roy staggered across the street to his wagon. After two failed attempts, he hauled himself onto the seat.

“Do you believe him?” Sean had left the saloon to join Noah.

“We’re going to find out.”

They walked together to the boardinghouse. The restaurant was full, Suzanne moving from table to table. Spotting them, she motioned them to an empty table. When Noah shook his head, she joined them.

“What do you need?”

“Do you have a boarder named Mick?”

"I do. I think he's upstairs. Do you want to talk to him?"

"Sure do. Outside would be best. Do you know his last name?" Noah asked.

"McNally."

"Thanks, Suzanne."

While she walked up the stairs, Sean and Noah waited outside. Within minutes, an older man with long, thinning brown and gray hair opened the door to the boardwalk. His steps stalled when his gaze landed on Sean.

"What do you want?"

"Come on outside so we can talk," Sean said.

Mick glanced behind him before closing the door. "You've been spreading rumors about me. Why?"

"They're the truth. My stallion died because of you."

Sean stepped forward. "I never treated your horse."

Mick glared at him. "May not have been you, but one just like you."

"Just like me?"

"You know. Self-righteous docs who say they know all about horses, but they don't. I ain't going to stand around and let you do the same to the fine folks in this town."

Sean glanced at Noah, who shrugged. "We've never met, have we?"

"Don't matter. I know your type. Think you know

everything. You don't know nothing."

Sean glared at him. "You best stop those tales, or we're gonna have serious trouble. My skills are proven. I run an honest practice, and I won't have you besmirching my name over some grudge."

Mick didn't respond, nor did he back down. "I can say whatever I want. You can't stop me."

"But I can." Suzanne stepped outside. "I heard what you said, Mick, and I want you out of your room."

"You can't do that," Mick growled.

"I can. You haven't paid for today, so I want you out within the hour. If you don't leave, I can assure you the sheriff will be glad to help get you out on the street."

Mick's face reddened as his breaths came in gasps. "Yeah, all right. I'll leave, but this ain't over."

Sean thanked Suzanne before turning on his heel, Noah following behind.

"Well, that's one rumor settled. But something tells me this isn't over yet."

Sean's face was stoic. "No, not until I've regained the full trust of this town."

Sean rose early the next morning, determined to start repairing the damage done to his reputation. After a quick breakfast, he loaded up his medical bag, tacked up his horse, and set off to visit the ranches and farms on the outskirts of town.

His first stop was the Wagner dairy farm. As Sean approached the small farmhouse, Mr. Wagner stepped outside, eyeing him warily.

"Morning, Mr. Wagner. I'm Sean MacLaren, the new veterinarian in town. I wanted to introduce myself and see if you have any animals in need of care."

Mr. Wagner looked hesitant. "I heard you treated the Pelletiers' cattle, but then there was talk..."

Sean held up a hand. "I know, and I aim to set the record straight. Those were vicious rumors spread by a man with a grudge. Until yesterday, I'd never met the man. I graduated top of my class from veterinary college in Edinburgh and my skills are proven."

He went on to describe some of his successful treatments back home. Mr. Wagner listened intently, his doubts easing.

"Well now, perhaps you could take a look at our old milk cow, Betsy. She's got a persistent limp I can't figure out."

"I'd be happy to," Sean said.

After examining Betsy, Sean determined the cause and recommended a treatment plan. Mr. Wagner beamed, shaking his hand vigorously.

"Much obliged for your help, Doc. You're welcome back here anytime."

Sean tipped his hat and set off, buoyed by the encounter. The realist in him knew it could be a long while before squelching the false rumor. All he could do was face it one ranch at a time.

Chapter Ten

Sean wiped the sweat from his brow during his ride back to town. It was a few hours after noon, and all he wanted was to relax for a bit. The day had been long but rewarding. He'd visited three more ranches and one farm, treating various ailments in horses, cattle, and another old cow.

Leaving his horse at the livery, he walked to the opposite end of town and his clinic. As he approached McCall's, he spotted Camilla through the window, sitting alone, nursing a cup of tea. He hesitated, then straightened his vest and strode inside.

"Afternoon, Camilla." He touched the brim of his hat. "Mind if I join you?"

Looking up in surprise, she gestured to a chair. "Please, have a seat."

She studied him over her teacup. "You look tired. Busy day?"

"It was, but a good kind of tired. I've been visiting ranches, trying to suppress those false rumors. I hope you didn't believe them."

Camilla smiled. "Noah told me about them this morning. I already knew you were a skilled veterinarian. The man who started them should be in jail."

Sean chuckled. "Well, I appreciate your confidence in me. Not sure about jail. I'll be glad when he leaves town."

"Noah told me he rode out this morning."

"Coffee, Doc?" Betts stood beside their table.

"Yes, please. Do you still have any of your delicious rolls?"

"Two left."

"I'll take both. Thanks, Betts."

He looked back at Camilla. "I was wondering if you'd care to join me for supper this evening? I'd like to hear more about growing up in New York."

Her eyes lit up. "Supper would be lovely."

"Wonderful. I'll be at your place at six to escort you to the Eagle's Nest. I mean...assuming six is good for you."

"It's perfect."

Sean grinned, thanked Betts as she set down his coffee and rolls, and tucked into his food.

Camilla checked the mirror in her bedroom a few minutes before six, pleased with the simple yet elegant blue dress. Sean's knock came a few minutes later.

She opened the door to see him cleaned up and wearing a tailored jacket and tie. His gaze wandered over her with an appreciative grin.

"You look beautiful, Camilla."

"Thank you. You look wonderful yourself, Doctor."

His chuckle caused her stomach to flutter. "Are you ready?"

"Let me get my wrap." She returned a moment later, closed the door behind her, and slipped an arm through his.

Over elk steaks and potatoes, Sean recounted his studies at the Edinburgh veterinarian college. "It was tough, but I'm glad I stuck it out. My uncle, Ewan, had a lot of reservations about me leaving. He said ranching was the only life for a MacLaren. I told him there was no reason I couldn't do both. Between my father and cousins, he relented."

"Understandable. I'm sure a ranch the size of your family's requires a large number of men."

"It does, and the family hires a lot of ranch hands. What was your life like, Camilla?"

"What you'd expect from the oldest daughter of a wealthy businessman. My father wanted me to marry well in New York. But I craved adventure. When Cole visited, intending to return to Splendor, I made up my mind to follow him. I'm so glad I listened to my heart and not cave to social obligations."

Sean smiled, holding up his glass of wine. "To forging our own paths." They clinked glasses.

The conversation flowed with an ease Sean had never experienced with another woman. Not that there'd been many. He'd left for Scotland early, spending the years attending classes and studying. Camilla was witty and well-read. Sean found himself laughing often, despite his initial shyness.

After dessert, they strolled through town as the sun set. "Thank you for supper. It's been ages since I've enjoyed an evening out."

"My pleasure." Sean hesitated. "I know it's forward, but I'd like to do this again."

Camilla met his gaze. "I'd like that, too."

They walked back to her house, both reluctant for the evening to end.

He watched as she disappeared inside, not ready to leave. Though he didn't want to believe it, there was something special between them.

As Sean walked back to the clinic, his mind swirled with thoughts of Camilla. The future felt bright and full of possibilities.

The streets of Splendor were alive with activity on the morning of July 4th. Colorful banners fluttered in the breeze while the smells of roasted corn, apple pie, and sizzling steaks drifted through the air. Children chased each other, their laughter ringing above the band's music. Couples spun across the wooden dance floor erected in the town square while others clapped along to the tunes.

Sean stood back from the festivities, leaning

against a hitching post as he observed the scenes of merriment around him. A tap on his shoulder made him turn. He was surprised to see Camilla standing there, a shy smile on her face.

"Fancy a game of horseshoes?" She gestured toward the pit nearby. They'd shared a memorable meal a week earlier. With his busy schedule, he hadn't yet planned a second supper invitation.

She held out her hand. "Bet I can beat you."

Sean slipped his hand into hers. "Well, when you put it that way, I can hardly refuse."

As the game commenced, they fell into a friendly rhythm. He took pleasure in her quiet concentration before each throw, the way she cheered his good shots, and how she laughed off her own errant tosses. Though neither were experts, they were well-matched.

"We make a fine team," he commented as her metal shoe clanked around the stake. She smiled in response.

Continuing their game, Sean found himself observing the woman at his side. There was a grace to her, despite the simple gingham dress she wore. And when she spoke, though her words were few, they were insightful and kind.

Around them, the festivities carried on in full swing. Children laughed and played simple games of quoits and sack races, while couples continued dancing to the lively music. The tantalizing scents of roasted meats and fresh baked pies drifted from the food stalls lining the street, where locals exchanged friendly greetings and enthusiastic handshakes.

He was focused on the horseshoe game at hand. Camilla's competitive spirit revealed itself in her determination to outscore him. Yet it was a friendly rivalry, without malice or arrogance.

"Come now, Sean, you'll have to do better than that if you hope to defeat me," she teased as another of Sean's throws went wide.

"I suppose I'll have to be content with second place today."

As the morning wore on, he realized how at ease he felt in Camilla's company. The initial hesitance between them, after meeting weeks earlier, had shifted into camaraderie, and possibly more.

After a few more rounds, Sean's stomach began to rumble.

"I don't know about you, but I could use a bite to eat after all this activity."

Camilla nodded in agreement.

They made their way over to the food stalls, the sumptuous aromas growing stronger with each step. He purchased two generously sized portions of roasted beef for himself, and a chicken potpie for her.

As they ate, he was approached by a grizzled older man with a thick beard. "I hear you're a veterinarian."

He wiped his mouth, extending his hand in greeting. "Sean MacLaren. Pleased to make your acquaintance."

"Name's Jeb Stokes. I've got a ranch a few miles outside of town. One of my horses has come up lame, and I'm at my wit's end trying to figure out what's wrong with him."

Sean's eyes lit up at the prospect of being able to utilize his skills. "I'd be more than happy to come take a look, Mr. Stokes. We can ride out now if you want."

"Tomorrow is fine. Morning is best." The rancher gave him directions. "Early. Seven all right?"

"I'll be there."

Several other locals approached with their own animal concerns. Everyone from an elderly milk cow with mastitis to a prized sheep dog with a strange skin condition. Sean listened, assuring them he would do his best to remedy their animals' afflictions.

When they returned to the games and contests, he felt buoyed by the conversations with locals. For the first time since arriving in Splendor, he believed this town held his future.

Camilla proved herself an adept and spirited competitor at the three-legged race, pie eating contest, and sack race. Laughter rang out between them as they good-naturedly teased each other over their mishaps and minor defeats.

When Sean stumbled during the wheelbarrow race, sending her sprawling into the dirt, he was sure she'd be furious. Instead, she rose, brushed herself off, and fixed him with a wry grin. He smiled back, relieved she hadn't taken offense.

Camilla glanced at Sean, noticing how the fading light softened his sharp features. "I haven't had this much fun in...well, I can't remember when."

Sean stopped, turning to face her. The depth of emotion in his eyes made her breath catch. "Camilla, I..." He paused, searching for the right words. "Today meant a lot to me, too. More than you know."

Camilla's heart fluttered at the intimacy of the moment. Though a part of her resisted, she found herself drawn to this complex man beside her.

"How about a walk?"

She linked her arm through his. As they made their way back to the town square, the sound of music and laughter grew louder. Lanterns and strings of lights illuminated the scene as dusk settled over Splendor.

Looking around, he spotted Cole waving them over to a crowded table. As they wove through the crowd, a young boy darted past, bumping hard into Camilla. Stumbling, she cried out, losing her balance.

Sean's arm shot out, snagging her around the waist, breaking her fall. They ended up pressed together, faces inches apart. Her eyes widened. Sean's heart hammered in his chest.

"You all right?"

She nodded, flustered at the closeness. For a heated moment, they remained frozen, the noise of the crowd fading away.

Then Cole appeared, frowning at the disheveled pair. "Everything okay over here?"

They sprung apart, the spell broken. Sean rubbed the back of his neck. "Just, uh...a little accident. No harm done."

Cole's eyes narrowed, but he said nothing more.

Sean sat at the crowded table, trying to focus on the conversation flowing around him. His thoughts kept drifting back to the heated moment with Camilla. The feeling of her slender frame pressed against him, her startled eyes gazing up into his.

Glancing at her now, he noticed a faint blush still staining her cheeks whenever their eyes met. She laughed at something Lena Evans said, though the smile didn't light up her eyes.

Cole sat on his sister's other side, wearing a perpetual scowl as his sharp gaze darted between them. Sean's stomach knotted with unease. Clearly, Camilla's overprotective brother had noticed the sparks between them.

As the afternoon stretched on, Sean tried to act normal, chatting with ranchers about the promising summer grass and his veterinary practice. But his thoughts kept circling back to Camilla.

By the time evening fell, Sean was wound tight. He wanted to get her alone, talk about what happened. As the crowd began to thin, he seized his chance.

"Walk with me?"

They strolled away from the crowd. Reaching the stables, Sean stopped, turning to face her. He took a deep breath.

"Camilla, about earlier, I..."

She pressed a finger to his lips, stopping his words. "I know," she whispered. Before he could react, she stood on her toes and brushed her mouth against his in a feather light kiss.

For an instant, Sean was stunned. Then, unable to resist, he crushed her in his arms and kissed her hungrily. She melted against him with a tiny moan that ignited his blood.

They broke apart, breathless. Camilla touched her mouth, eyes wide.

"Sean, I..."

A shout interrupted her. Cole strode toward them, face mottled with rage.

"Get your hands off my sister!"

Chapter Eleven

Cole grabbed Sean roughly by the shoulders, wrenching him away from Camilla.

Raising his hands, Sean tried to calm the situation. He'd never known his friend to have a quick temper. Had never seen him this angry.

"Easy, Cole. No need for trouble."

Cole pulled back a fist, but Camilla jumped between them.

"Stop it!" She turned pleading eyes toward her brother. "You don't understand. I care for Sean. Deeply."

Her brother's face twisted, though his rage appeared to fade. "Have you lost your senses? Do you have any idea how much younger he is than you?" The instant the words left his mouth, Cole knew he'd made a huge mistake.

Camilla's eyes flashed, first in astonishment, then in hurt. She shook her head as words died in her throat.

"Her age means nothing to me." Sean reached for her hand. She pulled it away, taking a step back. The gesture disturbed him.

Taking a deep breath, Cole shook his head as he exhaled. "I'm sorry, Cam. I just...well, I don't want to see you get hurt again." Turning, he stalked away into the growing darkness.

They stood several feet apart, neither speaking as Cole's solid form disappeared around a corner. Reaching out again, this time, she allowed him to thread his fingers through hers.

"What did he mean?"

"I think my brother was clear." She looked away, then at the ground. "I'm older than you."

"Not about that. As I said, your age means nothing to me."

"It should. If not now, then…" Camilla realized she was getting much too far ahead of herself. "He's right. This can't go anywhere." She pulled her hand away from his.

"It's too early to know where this will go. My hope is—"

"Stop, Sean. Just stop, please." The life seemed to seep out of her. Typical of Camilla, she straightened her spine, meeting his gaze. "You should find someone closer to your age."

A thin smile appeared on his face as he inched toward her. "I've already found the woman I want."

"You can't know that. It's too soon."

"You're not going to argue with me on this, are you?"

"I don't know. Maybe. Well…yes."

This time, the smile reached his eyes. "Come here."

Shaking her head, she took a step backward.

"Camilla. Come here, please."

She took a small step closer, then edged back, knowing what the future would hold if she didn't walk away. Her chest squeezed as a slice of the past gripped her heart. She'd vowed to never set herself up for the same devastating hurt again.

"I'm sorry. Cole's right. This can't go any further." Her eyes softened, replaced with a quiet pleading. "I hope we can remain friends."

Before Sean could respond, or try to stop her, she'd hurried down the street.

Sunlight crept through the curtained windows of Sean's home, which doubled as his veterinary clinic. The first glimmers of dawn did little to ease the weight that pressed upon his chest, a physical manifestation of the restless night he'd endured. He lay there on the mattress, an arm flung over his eyes, the blankets tangled around his legs.

His mind was a frenzied sea, the same as he'd seen in the ocean off San Francisco. The waves crashed against the shore, just like each memory of Camilla. The way her hair caught the sunlight, or how her laugh could fill a room with warmth. Now, those memories were tinged with the bitterness of her sudden departure from his life.

He pushed himself up, swinging his legs to the side. His feet landed on the cold, wooden floor, reminding him another day had begun. The second day without the comfort of Camilla's friendship.

He splashed water onto his face from the basin atop his dresser, the coolness shocking him awake. Sean gazed at his reflection in the small mirror propped against the wall, noting the stubble shadowing his jaw and the dark circles under his eyes. There was work to be done, animals in need of care. Today, his heart pulled him toward a different task.

He dressed in his usual attire—a white shirt, waistcoat, and sturdy trousers. Pulling on boots and grabbing the well-worn hat which had taken him from Scotland to California, then to Montana, he strapped his gunbelt around his waist.

Sean stepped out into the early morning, the town of Splendor coming to life around him. The dirt streets, the wooden storefronts with their painted signs, all seemed unchanged, yet everything felt different without Camilla.

With purpose in his stride, he made his way toward the sheriff's office, the sound of his boots thudding against the wood planks of the boardwalk. Each step moved him closer to Cole, closer to the answers he sought.

The door to the sheriff's office loomed ahead. Sean's heart pounded as he reached for the handle, the metal cool and unyielding beneath his fingers. He drew in a deep breath, mustering every ounce of courage before stepping inside, relaxing when he spotted one deputy and no one else.

"Sean. What brings you by so early?" Cole's voice held no trace of welcome, just surprise at the unexpected visit.

"I need to speak with you about Camilla." His words were clipped with urgency. The air between them thickened.

"It's not my place to speak for Cam," Cole replied. "You should speak with her."

"I would, except she's cut me from her life. At least for now."

"Then there's nothing more to say." He leaned forward, resting his arms on the desk.

Moving forward, Sean grabbed a chair, lowering himself into it. "You opened this up, and you're the one who's going to explain what you meant. You both seem to think I care about a difference in age. I don't."

"Do you know how much younger you are than her?"

"No, and I don't care."

Cole's eyes narrowed. "By my calculation, there's nine years between you."

Sean knelt beside the ailing calf, his hands gentle yet firm as they palpitated the tender belly. The mother cow loomed close, her eyes wide and watchful. She didn't interfere with ministrations.

"Easy, girl," he soothed, both to the calf and its mother. The trust the animals placed in him was humbling. Here, in the straw-laden barn with the scent of hay and earth mingling in the air, Sean found a measure of peace.

He'd ridden out of Splendor shortly after his discussion with Cole. Camilla's brother had surprised him by estimating nine years separated Sean and his sister.

Nine years wasn't insurmountable, though a bigger difference than he'd thought. His guess had been four, maybe five. Thanking Cole, Sean had left, taking the long way back to his house as he thought of his next steps.

He'd always planned on children. The news of Camilla's age put her in more peril during a pregnancy than younger women. Enough peril to forego having the family he'd envisioned. Could he go through life without the children he'd imagined?

"Reckon she'll pull through, Doc?" Teddy Minor leaned on the fence, his weathered face creased with concern.

"Give her a couple of days, plenty of fluids, and keep her warm. If the calf won't take milk from the mother, you'll have to feed it by hand. If you do, there's a good chance your calf will make it."

Sean stood, brushing dirt from his knees. He packed away a syringe and bottle of medicine into his leather bag, catching Teddy's nod of gratitude.

"Can't thank you enough. You sure have a way with beasts, Doc."

"Animals don't ask for much, just care and understanding." Sean's words held a trace of wistfulness, the subtext clear in his own mind. Animals were unlike people, who were a far more complicated breed.

The day lengthened, shadows stretching across the landscape as Sean made his way from ranch to ranch. At each stop, his heart worked double time as he healed his four-legged patients while wrestling with thoughts of Camilla.

"Doc, this one's been wheezing something fierce." Another rancher, Tom Ellis, informed him what he'd observed.

"Let's take a look, Tom."

As dusk approached, Sean rode back to Splendor. His muscles screamed for rest, and his eyelids felt as if they were lined with lead. Yet it wasn't the promise of his own bed spurring him on. It was thoughts of Camilla and what he'd do next.

He couldn't shake the image of her, proud and resolute, walking away from what they'd started to build together. And what did Cole mean by *again*? *"I don't want to see you get hurt again."*

Sean craved answers, not sure if he'd ever get them. As he dismounted and led his horse to the stable, his resolve hardened. Come morning, he'd knock on Camilla's door and hope she answered.

Sean settled into his bed, the fatigue of the day heavy upon his limbs. Closing his eyes didn't result in sleep. Camilla's face danced behind his lids, and the weight of unanswered questions pressed down on him.

The night stretched long and unforgiving around Sean as he lay in the bed of his modest house, both his livelihood and sanctuary. Despite the exhaustion tugging at every muscle, sleep remained a stranger, kept at bay by the tumultuous thoughts churning within him.

He turned onto his side, the bed creaking under his weight. A picture of Camilla popped into his thoughts, her slender form wrapped in determination. Her graceful walk. A woman who knew her own mind.

At last, Sean's thoughts blurred into the murky haze of sleep, images and conversations weaving dreams offering no solace.

The first blush of morning spilled through the window, chasing away shadows and painting the room in soft hues. Sean stirred, a subtle shift from the realm of dreams to the stark reality of daybreak. With the new light came clarity, a sharpening of purpose slicing through the fog of uncertainty.

He rose, muscles protesting, joints popping against the onslaught of another day. There was no time for dawdling. Today, he was a man on a mission. The soft murmur of town life reached his ears as he dressed and stepped outside.

Sean approached the familiar wooden house, so

similar to his own. He paused at the door, hand raised to knock, the moment stretching at his hesitation. With a breath drawn deep, Sean knocked, the sound echoing.

When he received no response, he knocked again. Standing still, he listened for a sign she was inside. None came.

Disappointed, he retraced his steps, crossing Frontier Street to the St. James. Taking the steps, he nodded at Michael, the hotel manager, before scanning the dining room.

"May I help you, Doc?"

"I'm looking for Miss Santori. Have you seen her this morning?"

"Sorry, I haven't."

"Guess I'll keep looking." Recrossing the street, he checked through the front window of McCall's. She wasn't there, either. Hunger clawed at his insides, but he refused to eat until he found her.

Walking to the sheriff's office, he ducked inside, glad to see Deputy Coulter at the desk. "Good morning, Cash."

"Sean. Have a seat and tell me what can I do for you?"

He did as Cash said, taking a seat. Looking at the stove, he was about to pour a cup of coffee when the door crashed against the wall, sending a jolt through him as if lightning had struck the earth beneath his feet. He and Cash snapped their attention to the imposing figure framed by the doorway.

"Gabe," Cash uttered, his voice low and threaded with curiosity.

The sheriff of Splendor stood there, his usual composure scorched away by a blaze of urgency in his eyes. His hat was clutched in one hand, his chest heaving from exertion or perhaps emotion. The badge on his chest glinted ominously, as though it foretold trouble brewing on the horizon.

"Sean." Gabe addressed him directly, his tone carrying the sharp edge of command. "I've been looking for you. You need to come with me. Now. It's Camilla."

Sean's heart stalled, then galloped like a wild mustang across the plains. "What happened?"

"Can't say for certain. She's at the clinic with Doc McCord."

Without another word, Sean swept past Gabe, his long strides eating up the ground between himself and the clinic. He could hear Gabe behind him, but he didn't slow. His world had narrowed down to the image of Camilla—strong, unyielding Camilla—in distress.

As they approached the clinic, a hush seemed to fall over the town of Splendor, as if even the buildings and dusty streets sensed the gravity of the moment.

"Doc!" Sean called out as he entered the clinic, his voice echoing against the whitewashed walls. "Where is she?"

Dr. Clay McCord emerged from one of the exam rooms, his expression grave. "In here. She's stable for now, but—"

Chapter Twelve

"Stable?" Sean interrupted, his words clipped with fear and a hint of anger. "What happened? Is she hurt?"

"Easy, now," Dr. McCord soothed, placing a firm hand on Sean's shoulder. "She took a nasty fall from her horse. Seems like she was out riding by herself. Got thrown when her mount spooked at a rattler. She called out for you before drifting off about thirty minutes ago."

"Let me see her."

Clay led Sean through the doorway where Camilla lay. Her face was pale, a stark contrast to her usually vibrant complexion, and a bandage was wrapped tightly around her head. Yet, even in her unconscious state, she radiated a formidable presence. He didn't notice Cole leaning against a counter until he almost ran into him.

Their eyes met, though neither spoke as Sean approached the bed, his heart thrumming painfully against his ribs. He reached out to brush a stray lock of hair from her forehead. His touch was feather light.

"Camilla? I'm here, Camilla."

He took her hand in his, repeating her name again.

"Sean..." Her voice was a mere wisp of sound.

"I'm right here, Camilla."

"Sean..."

"Shh, don't try to speak." Sean squeezed her hand, his rugged features softening with affection and relief. "Just rest now. I'm here."

"Her color is returning." Cole's voice from beside him was laced with a brother's worry.

"Do you know what happened?"

"Only what Doc McCord told me. I'm thankful she wasn't too far from town when it happened. A cowboy found her and brought Camilla here. He didn't stick around."

"She's determined to take on the world alone."

"Perhaps." Cole stepped closer to his sister. "She's always been stubborn. Maybe you'll be the one to convince her relying on others isn't a weakness."

Their gazes locked, an unspoken understanding passing between them. The silence enveloping the small room was broken by a knock on the door.

The door creaked open, Sean's eyes narrowed as he recognized Deputy Morgan Wheeler standing in the doorway.

"Sorry to interrupt, but Gabe sent me to get you, Cole."

"Can't it wait?" Cole's tone was sharp, protective instincts flaring for his sister who lay vulnerable in the bed.

"Afraid not," Morgan replied with a grimace. "It's the Jenkins homestead. They've been hit hard by rustlers. Lost nearly half their herd. Old man Jenkins took a bullet."

Cole glanced between Camilla and Morgan, torn between duty and family.

"Go," Sean said. "I'll stay with her. She won't be alone."

"Thank you." Cole's voice had softened with gratitude.

Sean looked down at Camilla, her breathing even and calm, unaware of the turmoil around her.

"Who would do such a thing?" Sean's hands fidgeted with the edge of the blanket, his gaze still on the closed door. "Rustling's one thing, but shooting a man..."

"Money makes folks do terrible things," came a weak reply.

Sean's head snapped to the bed, meeting Camilla's now open eyes. "You should be resting."

"Can't sleep... Too much noise in my head." She tried to sit up. Sean's hands were there in an instant, gentle but firm, easing her back.

"Shh, just lie still. You need your strength."

"Strength seems to be failing me."

"Never." Sean smiled down at her. "You're the strongest person I know, Camilla Santori. Don't you forget that."

Camilla's hand squeezed his before her body relaxed into sleep once more.

Sean was just about to drag a chair next to the bed

when the door to the exam room swung open. Doc McCord strode in, his face creased with concern.

"Sorry to interrupt, but a rider arrived from the Pelletier ranch. I believe it's urgent."

"What is it?"

"The ranch hand said Rachel's horse is severely lame. She isn't sure what it is, and doesn't know how to treat it. Dax asked you to ride right away."

Sean hesitated, glancing back at Camilla, who hadn't woken. As much as he wanted to stay, he knew his duty to injured animals came first.

"I'll return as soon as I can," he told Clay.

The doctor nodded and ducked out of the room to alert the nurse.

With great reluctance, Sean stood and left the room, his mind on the horse awaiting his aid.

Sean hurried to the livery to ready his horse. He rode to his office to repack his bag before urging the animal into a brisk gallop as he set off for the Pelletier ranch.

The afternoon wind whipped through Sean's hair as he leaned low over the horse's neck, coaxing all the speed he could out of the galloping animal. His medical bag bounced about, reminding him of the urgent task ahead.

As the horse's hooves pounded down the road, his thoughts kept returning to Camilla. He hated leaving her alone and in pain at the clinic, but knew McCord and Carrie MacKenzie would provide her with the best possible care while he was gone.

Squinting against the setting sun, Sean crested a hill, spotting the Pelletier ranch in the distance.

He reined his horse to a stop outside the large barn, the smell of hay and horses enveloping him. From inside came the sounds of whinnying and snorting as the animals settled in for the night. Then he heard the sound of a horse in deep distress.

Dismounting, he retrieved his medical bag and hurried into the barn. Spotting Rachel and Dax, he recognized their faces were etched with concern.

"Thank you for coming so quickly." Dax shook Sean's hand. His eyes were tired but determined. "Rachel's mare came up lame this afternoon. There's more pain than you'd expect. It's nothing I remember seeing. We've got her in a stall."

"Let's take a look."

They led him to a spacious stall housing a beautiful Pinto mare. The horse bobbed her head anxiously, keeping weight off its left hind leg. Sean let the mare catch his scent before moving closer.

"What's her name?"

"Dancer," Rachel responded.

"Easy, Dancer." Sean ran a gentle hand along the horse's flank. With an expert eye, he examined the injured leg, feeling for swelling or heat. The mare flinched when Sean probed near her hoof.

"She has thrush. See here?"

Rachel and Dax looked where he pointed. "It

smells." Rachel grimaced. "Is it painful?"

Sean set the hoof down with care. "Very painful. The hoof infection causes the discharge, which is what you smell. It'll progress if not addressed."

Rachel let out a breath. "So you can fix her up, Doctor?"

Sean met her worried gaze. "I believe so. I'll need to thoroughly clean her hoof before applying a copper sulfate solution. It'll dry out and disinfect the hoof. I'll leave enough for you to reapply four times a day. I fully expect that treatment to work. I'll be back tomorrow morning to check on her again. Sometimes, zinc sulfate works if for some reason the copper sulfate doesn't."

He spoke in low, soothing tones as he worked on the mare, keeping the horse calm despite the pain. Once the abscess was clean, he applied the antiseptic. Dancer lifted her head and whinnied as Sean poured the solution over the wound. "I know it stings, girl, but we've got to keep it clean."

Bandaging the wound with strips of cloth, Sean continued talking to the mare. After a while, her muscles relaxed under his steady hands.

When the strips of cloth were secured, he rose and stepped away. "The solution will help draw out the infection. Even when the hoof appears healed, I'd suggest not riding her for several more days."

Rachel relaxed. "I can't thank you enough. Dancer was a present from Dax years ago."

Dax shook Sean's hand again. "We're obliged,

Sean. You're welcome to stay for supper."

"Thanks for the offer, but I need to get back."

Dax nodded. "Get home safe."

Sean's mind was filled with concern for Camilla as he rode back to town. Though the sun was beginning to set, he went straight to the clinic to check on her.

Quietly entering her room, Sean was relieved to see Camilla sleeping peacefully. Her face still bore scrapes from the fall, but the pained expression he'd last seen was gone.

Nurse Carrie looked up from her chair by the bedside. "She's doing much better. The laudanum helped with the pain and is allowing her to rest."

Sean nodded, brushing a strand of hair from Camilla's face. She stirred at his touch. Her eyes fluttered open, giving him a drowsy smile.

"You came back," she murmured.

"Of course. Did you think I wouldn't?"

Her smile widened before her eyes drifted closed again. Sean stayed a moment longer, watching the steady rise and fall of her chest. Then, with a reluctant sigh, he left to catch a few hours of sleep before dawn.

Morning came too soon, a rooster's crow spurring Sean from bed. After a hasty breakfast, he walked to the clinic. Camilla was sitting up, chatting with the nurse. Her face lit up when he entered the room. Carrie excused herself, giving them privacy.

"Good morning, Sean.”

“How are you feeling?"

"Much better." Camilla reached for his hand, threading her fingers through his.

"Sore. The laudanum helps."

"You gave us quite a scare. Doc said other than the head injury and sprained left wrist, there are no broken bones. Just cuts and bruises that will heal quickly. It’s a miracle you weren't more seriously injured."

He squeezed her hand, her fingers slender and delicate. He watched her in silence for a long moment, the air between them suddenly electric.

"I'm glad you’re here."

Sean met her gaze, seeing the veiled emotion there. "So am I."

Chapter Thirteen

Gabe Evans sat at his desk a few days later, telegram in hand. The news from Sheriff Parker Sterling in Big Pine made his gut twist.

One of his deputies had overheard a group of men discussing a bank robbery. They'd discussed snagging a woman who'd gotten away the last time. Sterling thought of Gabe and the warning he'd sent about a band of outlaws who'd tried kidnapping a local woman before being driven off.

Gabe sprang into action. Gathering all his deputies, he sent word for Noah Brandt, Nick Barnett, doctors Clay McCord and Drake Ralston, and Sean MacLaren to meet at the sheriff's office.

Within the hour, everyone had assembled, straining the capacity of his office. Gabe's face was grim as he explained about the outlaws who'd attempted to kidnap Camilla were planning a bank robbery in Splendor.

"It's only a matter of time before those snakes slither into Splendor," he said. "We need a plan to stop them."

Noah stroked his stubbled jaw. "We could set a trap. Stage an ambush outside town."

Cole shook his head. "It could work. We'd need an idea of when they're coming."

"I agree," said Deputy Beau Davis. "They could show in one day, five days, or a month from now."

Cash Coulter's eyes narrowed on the crude map spread out on Gabe's desk. "No different from us being prepared for them to show in town. We'll be watching for them to ride in."

"We could rotate deputies at a spot about half a mile from town," Deputy Shane Banderas said. "Set a signal system. Couldn't hurt, and it would be an early warning for those of us waiting here."

The men volleyed ideas back and forth, debating the best course of action. Sean listened quietly, weighing each suggestion.

Finally, the suggestions slowed. Gabe recited the options, letting them know which made sense to him. The others voiced their agreement. One by one, they pledged their support.

Noah grasped Gabe's shoulder. "You know I've got your back."

He gave his childhood friend a sharp nod. "And I've got yours."

Nick tipped his hat. "Those outlaws won't know what hit 'em once we're through."

"All right, let's get to work," Gabe said. "We've got a town to protect."

The men nodded, moving to gather what they needed from ammunition crates in the back. As they dispersed, the men spread the word around town, warning people of the potential danger. Clay McCord and Drake Ralston returned to the clinic to confirm their supplies if a shootout occurred.

A heavy silence fell over the town. Mothers herded children indoors while merchants near the bank boarded up windows. An air of uneasy anticipation settled like a shroud. Everyone believed if the outlaws returned, it would be soon.

From his perch on the ridge, Deputy Dutch McFarlin kept his keen eyes trained on the horizon. His jaw was set in a hard line, rifle resting casually across his lap. Though he maintained an aura of calm, his heart hammered a fierce rhythm against his ribs. He would not let harm come to this town or its people. Not while there was breath left in his body.

A hundred yards away, Deputy Zeke Boudreaux did the same. In twelve hours, two deputies would take their place. The rotation would continue until the outlaws appeared.

At the livery, Noah methodically loaded cartridges into his revolver, doing the same with his trusted Spencer repeating rifle. The Sharps rifle was already loaded, resting against a wall in the livery. His tense face was creased in concentration, hands moving with steady purpose. Satisfied with his preparations, he swung up onto his waiting horse. Gathering the reins, he touched his heels to the animal's flanks and loped toward the home he shared with his wife, Abby, and their children. He'd explain the situation before riding back to town.

Gabe's footsteps echoed on the deserted boardwalk as he made his final patrol of the town. An eerie silence pervaded, broken only by the mournful creak of a shop sign swinging in the breeze. His keen gaze swept the vacant streets, alert for any signs of movement. Satisfied things were secured, he turned his boots toward the sheriff's office.

Inside, he found Lena waiting, her lovely face creased with worry. At his entrance, she turned, relief flashing across her features.

"Everyone's safely tucked away," Gabe assured her, his voice a soothing rumble. He knew their children were safe at home with his father, Walter, watching over them. "We've done all we can to prepare. Now we batten down and hope for the best."

Lena's loaded rifle rested against an edge of her husband's desk. "I know you've done your best. I just pray it will be enough."

Gabe crossed the room and folded her into a fierce embrace. Lena clung to him, drawing strength from the solid breadth of his chest. After a long moment, he pressed a kiss to her hair and stepped back.

"Stay at home with Father and the children. If things go bad, you get everyone to the root cellar and bar the door. All right?" His hazel eyes bored intently into hers until she nodded. With a final caress of her cheek, he strode for the door. "If these are the outlaws

Sheriff Sterling suspects, they have a history of killing men, women, and children. They're without conscience or soul."

Lena nodded again. "I'll keep the children safe. You take care of the town."

He kissed her cheek, watched as she mounted her horse, reining it toward home.

Gabe waited until she was out of sight before he swung up onto his midnight black stallion. As he gathered the reins, Sean appeared leading his large, gray gelding. The younger man's jaw was set, green eyes hard with determination. He mounted up beside the sheriff, rifle in its scabbard. Together, they headed toward the edge of town to take up their positions.

Gabe and Sean rode in silence, the only sounds the rhythmic drumming of hooves and the creak of saddle leather. As they approached the meeting point, Gabe glanced over at his companion.

"I appreciate you volunteering for this, Sean. You being a newcomer to town and all."

He nodded, eyes scanning the horizon. "I suppose wherever a man lays his hat is home. In my short time here, Splendor's been good to me. I aim to repay the favor."

Gabe grinned, impressed by the younger man's grit. Before he could respond, Nick and Noah rode up to join them, rifles held at the ready. Gabe outlined the plan. Noah and Sean would take up positions on the north side of town while he and Nick covered the south. With terse nods, the men split off, spreading out to their assigned posts.

Gabe and Nick picketed their horses in a stand of scrub pine and bellied down atop a ridge overlooking the road to town. As the afternoon shadows lengthened, a taut silence fell between them. Gabe's thoughts turned to Lena, picturing her beautiful face creased with worry. He vowed to keep her safe, no matter the cost.

Beside him, Nick checked his rifle for the dozenth time, movements sharp with tension. Gabe knew the man's thoughts were also on his family's safety. Together, they kept their vigil, two old friends bound by duty and a bone-deep need to protect all they held dear.

Nick was the first to break the silence. "Quite a spot we're in, eh, Gabe?"

He grunted in agreement. "That it is. But you and I have seen worse."

Nick readjusted his grip on his rifle. "We have good men standing with us, Gabe. Noah is the best sharpshooter I've ever seen. MacLaren is solid. Your deputies are excellent. And the town's ready for a fight if it comes. We'll give those outlaws a fight if they dare show their faces."

Gabe tensed as a hawk's cry split the air. Scanning the terrain, he caught a hint of movement near a copse of trees. He tapped Nick's arm and pointed.

Wordlessly, they readied themselves, pulses quickening. They were as ready as they could be.

Nick and Gabe watched as the figure moved out from the trees. It was one of the deputies, Cash Coulter, riding back from his patrol.

Gabe let out a breath, lowering his rifle slightly.

They waited as Cash approached, his horse picking up speed. As he pulled up beside them, his expression was grim.

"The lookouts gave a signal. Riders coming up from the east. About a dozen strong. Moving fast and armed to the teeth. I'm betting they're our outlaw friends."

Gabe's jaw tightened as he raised his binoculars. After a moment, he spotted the riders, confirming what Cash reported. "Gather the others, tell them what you saw and have them get into position. If it's the outlaws, we'll make our stand as we planned."

With a sharp nod, Cash wheeled his horse around and took off back into town.

Nick looked to Gabe. "This will be a tough fight." His eyes blazed with cool determination.

"We'll give them a welcome they'll never forget." Gabe held up his binoculars, scanning the horizon once more. The sound of distant hoofbeats reached them. His mouth set in a hard line. "Here they come."

As planned, Gabe and Nick made their way back into town. The residents had barricaded themselves inside buildings and homes. An ominous silence had fallen over the town as people peeked out windows and doors, their weapons at the ready.

Gabe's gaze moved from south of Frontier Street to north, confirming his deputies had settled into their positions. Each gave a sharp nod as his gaze landed on them. He could see them checking their rifles and shotguns. Their faces etched with determination.

In the distance, the sound of galloping hooves grew louder. Noah joined them.

Gabe turned to Nick. "I want you and Noah on the rooftop there, pick them off from above." He pointed to the Dixie's flat roof overlooking the street.

"You got it," Nick said. He and Noah headed for the saloon's rear stairs.

Sean, on the balcony of the St. James Hotel, used his binoculars to watch the road from Big Pine. His pulse raced. He looked at Cole, who held a position across the street near the bank.

"Here they come!" Sean yelled. "I count close to twenty." He knew they'd believed there would be closer to a dozen.

Cole nodded, yelling the warning down the street.

In a thundering rush, over a dozen hard-looking men came charging straight into town, firing wildly as they bore down on the town. Gabe, his deputies, and several townsfolk fired from their protected positions.

The outlaws split apart, taking cover while keeping up a barrage of bullets.

From the saloon's rooftop, Nick and Noah picked off riders one by one. The street rang with gunshots and shouts. Gabe caught a glimpse of Cole hitting his mark, an outlaw toppling from his saddle. They were holding their ground, but the outlaws weren't stopping.

Gabe dove behind a wagon for cover as a hail of bullets kicked up dirt around him. He reloaded his revolver, the sounds of gunfire and men's shouts echoing down the street. Squinting through the dust, he spotted two outlaws attempting to flank Cole's position near the bank.

"Cut them off!" Gabe yelled to Morgan Wheeler. The young deputy nodded and scrambled farther down the alley, firing at the outlaws and driving them back.

From his higher vantage point, Noah continued picking off riders while Nick covered him. An outlaw took aim at the rooftop, and Noah rolled out of the way just in time as bullets peppered the spot where he'd been.

Again, Noah sighted along his rifle, aiming at a rider on a big bay, and squeezed the trigger. The outlaw toppled sideways off his horse.

"Good shot." Nick aimed and fired at another outlaw attempting to hide between two buildings.

Gabe looked up and down the street, his gaze locking on Deputy Caleb Covington, who was reloading behind a water trough across the street. "Do you see anyone?"

Caleb flinched as a bullet ricocheted off the water trough. He looked over the rim, dropping down when another bullet whizzed past his ear. Popping back up, he held a six-shooter in each hand, firing both between two buildings not far from where Gabe hid. Another outlaw screeched in pain before going silent.

Gabe stayed in place. They had the outlaws pinned down for now. He knew it was only a matter of time before their ammunition dwindled. This had to end soon.

Peering around the corner of the building, Gabe spotted who he believed was the outlaw leader. A big bear of a man, he hunkered down behind a wagon farther up the street.

"Keep me covered," Gabe yelled to Caleb.

Before his deputy could object, he spun out from the building's cover, firing his revolver as he charged up the street.

Bullets kicked up puffs of dirt around him as the outlaws tried to gun him down. He felt a sharp sting as one found its mark, tearing through the flesh of his upper arm. Gritting his teeth against the pain, he kept running.

The massive man rose up from behind the wagon, levering his rifle toward Gabe. Before he could fire, two shots rang out from behind Gabe. The outlaw's hat flew off his head before he roared in pain and dropped.

"I got you covered, boss!" Deputy Hex Boudreaux stared down from his position on the roof of Finn's saloon.

Gabe dove the last few feet to slide in behind the wagon next to the beefy outlaw. The man fumbled with his rifle as Gabe jammed his Colt into the outlaw's ribs.

"It's over. Tell your men to lay down their arms."

The man glared at him. For a moment, Gabe thought he might try to fight. Then his shoulders slumped.

"Hold fire!" The man shouted two more times to his gang. A few outlaws emerged from cover, hands in the air. Two swung into their saddles, kicking their horses in a race from town. A few shots hit the dirt around them before they rode out of range.

Gabe kept his gun trained on his prisoner until he was shackled. When Doc McCord came over to tend to the man's shoulder, Gabe shook his head in disbelief. They'd managed to beat back the outlaws without any lives lost on their side. It was a miracle.

With the adrenaline fading, Gabe became aware of the burning pain in his arm. Clay saw the blood and noticed him wince.

"You're next, Gabe." When he went to stand, Clay ordered him not to move. "Just a flesh wound. I'll get it cleaned and bandaged. You were lucky."

Gabe nodded, exhaling in relief. The sting of the bullet was nothing compared to what could've happened.

As Clay worked, Gabe's gaze drifted over the scene. Deputies were relieving the outlaws of their weapons and binding their hands. Beau Davis, Tucker Nolan, and Jonas Taylor were busy organizing the outlaws into a line to be escorted to the jail.

"There, all set." Clay tied off the bandage.

"Much obliged, Doc." Gabe rolled his sleeve down. He stood, wincing slightly at the pain, knowing his arm would be sore for a while.

"Don't overdo it with that arm," Clay advised. "Come see me tomorrow so I can change the dressing."

Gabe nodded. "Will do."

He turned to survey the town. People were venturing out into the streets, exchanging tearful hugs. The air buzzed with excitement and relief.

Chapter Fourteen

Sean stepped over the broken glass and splintered wood littering Frontier Street, surveying the aftermath of the chaotic shootout. Despite the exhaustion weighing on his shoulders, Sean knew he needed to check on Camilla.

Ever since she'd been thrown from her horse, he'd worried about her safety. Gritting his teeth against his weariness, Sean made his way down the dirt road toward her house. With each step, his boots kicked up small clouds of dirt, mirroring the swirling storm of emotions in his mind.

When he arrived at her door, a few minutes passed before she welcomed him inside. She moved gingerly due to her riding injury, her smile hidden behind uncertainty. Sean sat down at her table, comforted by the cozy atmosphere.

"I heard the gunfire." Her voice was edged with tension. "Is everyone all right?"

"The outlaws sustained the only casualties. A bullet grazed Gabe, but it was minor."

They sat in pensive silence for a moment, the weight of the day's events hanging over them. Sean knew Camilla was as stubborn and independent as him, but he vowed to keep her safe, no matter the cost.

She busied herself at the stove, the scent of simmering stew soon filling the small kitchen. He watched her work, noticing the care with which she tended the pot.

"Smells good." Sean hoped to lighten the mood. "My skills don't extend far past beans and biscuits."

Camilla laughed, the sound warm and melodic. "I suppose life out here requires some versatility in the kitchen. My family back east has servants for such things. I find it rewarding to fend for myself."

She brought two bowls of stew to the table, along with some bread and butter. Sean's mouth watered at the simple, hearty meal. As they ate, the conversation turned to recounting the day's events. He described the chaos of the shootout and its aftermath. She listened intently, her features sober as he spoke.

"It's all such a waste, Sean. The outlaws had to know the town would defend the bank."

He set down his spoon, contemplating her words. "The outlaws were driven by greed and nothing else. I don't believe they ever considered the strong defenses Gabe put in place."

Camilla nodded, stirring the remnants of her stew. "It seems the way out here, doesn't it?"

"It does. Remember, robbers and thieves live in every city from New York to San Francisco. Back east, your wealth shielded you from the dark actions in many parts of New York."

As the evening wore on, the conversation turned to

plans for the next day. Camilla mentioned her intention to ride out to the orphanage to bring supplies and check on the children.

"It's only a few miles south of town," she said. "I'll take it slow. The fresh air will do me good."

Sean hesitated, concern furrowing his brow. She'd been thrown from her horse just days before, suffering a head injury and sprained wrist.

"Are you sure that's wise? So soon after your fall? Perhaps you should give it a few more days."

"I'm not some China doll." Her voice held an edge that caught him off guard.

"That's not what I meant. I only want you to be safe."

"I don't need your protection." She rose from her chair. "I'm improving each day. And I'll remind you, I've been riding these trails for months."

Sean stood as well, stung by her sharp tone. "Forgive me for caring about you. I thought we were friends."

"Friends don't tell each other what to do." Fisted hands rested on her hips.

The two locked eyes, tension crackling between them. He saw the stubborn set of her jaw and knew further argument was futile.

"Clearly, I've overstepped. I'll leave you be."

Donning his hat, Sean walked out into the night, shaken by their sudden clash. Camilla watched the door close behind him, regret mingling with indignation. Each had asserted their independence, though at what cost?

Sean stepped into the cool night air, Camilla's sharp words still ringing in his ears. He'd only meant to express concern for her well-being. Instead, she'd bristled at any suggestion of weakness. Sighing, he strode down the quiet street, needing time alone to process their argument.

Despite her stubbornness, he couldn't shake his desire to protect her. There was a fragility beneath her fierce exterior, something she was determined to hide. Sean wished she'd let him in, but he wouldn't force the issue.

The raucous noise of the Dixie saloon beckoned him. Though he rarely drank, tonight, Sean craved the warm burn of whiskey. Pushing through the swinging doors, he found an empty spot at the bar. The boisterous crowd and clink of glasses faded into the background as he stared into his glass.

Camilla's face swam before him, her eyes flashing with her unique fire. He'd come to admire her strength and passion. Unfortunately, her sharp tongue could cut like a whip when roused. Did he truly want to be friends with a woman who could cut someone down with vicious retorts? He didn't know.

Sean tossed back the whiskey, feeling its soothing burn. Where did they go from here? He cared too much to walk away. Yet Camilla seemed determined to push him away. The whiskey soothed his damaged soul.

The raucous saloon faded into a grim haze. Tomorrow, he'd try again to see her. For now, he craved time alone to think.

Sean awoke with a start. He shot from his bed, rushing to look outside. All was calm and...normal. He realized the gunshots he heard were part of a dream and not a real threat.

As he blinked the sleep from his eyes, the lingering hurt from his argument with Camilla flooded back. Though his heart ached to see her, pride and doubt held him back.

With resolute focus, he packed his medical bag. Visiting the outlying ranches would keep his mind occupied. He'd always found solace in his work. The animals never judged or picked a fight.

After a quick breakfast, Sean walked to the livery, the crisp morning air filling his lungs. Saddling his horse, he wondered if Camilla was awake yet. Was she still intent on riding to the orphanage? Anxious energy coursed through him, but he tamped it down. She'd made her wishes clear.

The cool morning air helped clear Sean's mind as he set off toward the first ranch. Grasslands rippled in the breeze, dotted with bright wildflowers. He inhaled deeply, letting the scenic ride soothe his troubled thoughts. Out here, it was just him and nature's majesty.

By mid-morning, Sean reached the first ranch. He

was greeted by the owner, who showed him to the barn and nearby pasture. As he examined the horses and cattle, he felt the comfortable familiarity of his work wash over him.

The animals responded well to his gentle ministrations. Sean spoke soothing words as he treated their injuries and ailments. Though the work was tiring, he felt renewed purpose filling him. Here, he could heal and help. Here, he was needed.

For the rest of the day, he rode between ranches, caring for livestock. It was satisfying work, though his thoughts continued back to Camilla. He hoped she'd come to her senses and postponed the ride.

Knowing her audacious spirit, he worried she'd stubbornly stuck to her plan. As dusk fell, he turned his horse back toward town, conflicted about seeing her again after their harsh words.

Sean rode back into town as the sun sank below the horizon, casting long shadows across the street. He felt weary after a long day tending to animals.

Though he tried to lose himself in work, his thoughts kept returning to the heated argument between him and Camilla.

Replaying it in his mind, he thought of her indignant expression and defiant words. He hated leaving things so unpleasant between them.

As Sean guided his horse to the livery, he contemplated whether to stop by her house. The urge to check on her tugged at him. After her stern dismissal, would she even want to see him? Sighing, he dismounted and unsaddled his horse.

In the end, exhaustion won out over his conflicted emotions. He trudged home, each step heavier than the last. He longed for things to be easy between them again, knowing he couldn't force her to see reason or jeopardize her trust by being overbearing.

As Sean collapsed into bed, he tossed and turned most of the night. His mind churned with "what ifs" about Camilla riding while injured. He had to accept it was her choice to make, however foolish it seemed. As he drifted off to sleep, he hoped the new day would bring clarity and a chance to mend fences. For now, distance seemed the wisest choice.

Sean awoke the next morning feeling as conflicted as when he'd fallen into a fitful sleep. Though his body craved more rest, his mind raced ahead to the day before him. He rose and began his usual morning routine, though Camilla's image continued to plague him.

Had she ridden out to the orphanage so soon after her injury? He shook his head as he shaved, grimacing at the thought. She was brave to the point of recklessness. He had to find a way to make her see reason before she did something rash.

After dressing, Sean fixed breakfast, more

famished than he realized. As he ate, he contemplated walking the short distance to her house. He gave a slight shake of his head. The memory of their last bitter exchange gave him pause.

He'd never met a woman so determined to prove her independence. Admirable, though oftentimes reckless and frustrating. Sean sighed, hoping their clashing wills wouldn't drive an irreparable wedge between them. He'd come to care too much for Camilla to give up on her so easily.

Grabbing his hat, he began the short walk to her house. When it came into view, he gathered his courage. He hoped to make her understand his good intentions. His words came from caring, not from a desire to take control. Whether she heeded them or not, he prayed their bond would weather this dispute. With a deep breath, Sean stepped onto her porch and knocked.

When the door opened, he took what could be his one opportunity. "I had to come, to make sure you were all right."

She hesitated, one hand on her hip, facing him with a guarded expression. "As you can see, I'm fine. Now, if you'll excuse me, I'm expected back at the orphanage."

"Please, listen—" Sean began, but Camilla cut him off.

"No, you listen. I won't be mollycoddled like some fragile doll. What I do is my choice, risks included."

Her voice was sharp, but he detected a quavering undertone.

He softened his tone. "I know well your strength and independence. Still, everyone needs help at times."

She faltered, seeming to waver. Sean pressed his advantage and stepped closer, hands open in entreaty.

"Relax today. We can spend time together. If you must return to the orphanage, I'll borrow Noah's wagon and drive you."

Camilla searched his face, pride warring with humility. She understood the difference, knew she had too much of the first and too little of the last. Releasing a breath, a slow grin appeared.

"I'd enjoy spending time with you. On one condition."

One brow lifted. "What is that?"

"When we're finished for the day, you stay for supper. My way of repaying your kindness."

"It would be my honor." He offered his arm, and after a moment, Camilla took it, leaning into him as they walked inside.

Over the next few hours, they walked around town, stopping to peer into windows, and visit with people they knew. Sean stayed for a delicious supper of venison roast and fresh bread.

As darkness fell, and conscious of imposing too

long on her hospitality, Sean thanked her for a wonderful time. She walked him to the door, neither quite wanting to part ways.

On impulse, Sean reached out and squeezed her hand. Camilla's eyes widened in surprise, but she didn't pull away. Heart pounding, Sean hesitated, then leaned in as Camilla's lips parted in anticipation. He brushed his mouth against hers before releasing her hand.

"I should be on my way. Goodnight, Camilla."

"Goodnight, Sean." Her voice was tinged with regret.

As Sean walked away, he glanced back to see Camilla silhouetted in the doorway, watching him go. There was much still unresolved. Tonight had been a step in the right direction.

Sean took the long way home, walking through the quiet streets of Splendor. The brief kiss made his heart ache with longing and his head spin.

He decided to stop by the saloon for a nightcap, hoping to settle his restless mind. The Dixie was rowdy as usual, filled with raucous laughter and clinking glasses. Sean sat alone at the end of the bar, nodding to the bartender for a whiskey.

As he sipped his drink, the doors swung open and Gabe walked in. Spotting Sean, the sheriff ambled over, taking an open spot next to him.

"Evening, MacLaren."

Sean grunted, taking another swallow of whiskey.

"You have the look of a man with something on his mind."

Sean hesitated. He respected the sheriff, but was unsure how much to confess.

"It's about a woman," he admitted.

"Miss Camilla Santori."

Sean looked at him in surprise.

"The whole town's got eyes." Gabe chuckled before taking a sip of whiskey.

Sean flushed, chagrined. He turned to face him. "I want to court her proper. But I can't tell if she feels the same. We're so different..." He trailed off, uncertain of what to do next.

Gabe clasped him on the shoulder. "Trust me, she's sweet on you, too. I've seen the way she looks at you."

Sean felt a rush of hope. "You really think I've got a chance?"

"More than a chance. If you've got the guts to take it."

He arched a brow, pondering the sheriff's words. Gabe was right. It was time to take a risk.

Tossing back the last of his whiskey, Sean straightened. "Wish me luck."

Gabe grinned, saluting him with his glass.

With his spirits bolstered, Sean strode from the saloon. Tomorrow, he'd call on Camilla and make his intentions clear. It was time to discover if there was a chance for them after all.

Chapter Fifteen

Sean took a deep breath to steady his nerves as he approached Camilla's front door the next morning. He'd selected a clean shirt and his best coat, hoping to make a good impression. Raising his hand, he rapped several times before taking a step back.

After a moment, the door opened to reveal Camilla. Sean's heart leapt at the sight of her chestnut curls and sparkling green eyes.

"Sean. To what do I owe the pleasure?"

He removed his hat. "Miss Santori, I was hoping I might have a word with you."

She studied him for a moment before gesturing for him to enter.

"Please, come in."

He stepped inside, aware of her proximity in the cozy front room. She motioned for him to sit while she settled across from him.

"What did you wish to discuss?"

Setting his hat aside, he took a steadying breath. "These past weeks, I've come to care for you a great deal." Pausing, he held her gaze. "I know we come from different worlds, but I believe we have a chance to build a good life together. I'd like the chance to court you proper, if you'll permit me."

Camilla looked surprised, a becoming blush rising on her cheeks. Sean felt a pang of nervousness but forced himself to wait for the reply. Her features, open and curious, closed up, her bright eyes fading in disappointment. She straightened, as if she were about to address a room full of adults. When she spoke, her voice sounded dull, lifeless.

"I'm flattered, Sean. Truly, I am." She clasped her hands in her lap, staring down at them a moment before lifting her head. "It just isn't a good idea."

He sat stone still, her words registering, though they made no sense. "Explain to me why it isn't."

"There are a few reasons. The biggest being our age difference."

"Nine years doesn't matter to me."

"It should," she shot back.

"Why?"

"There are several reasons." Standing, she walked to the kitchen. Removing two cups from a cupboard, she filled each with coffee. Handing one to him, she walked to the front window, her back to him.

Setting his cup aside, he rose, moving behind her. When she didn't step away, he settled his hands on her shoulders, speaking in a low voice next to her ear.

"Tell me the reasons." He felt her shiver as his warm breath washed across her neck. She stepped away, his hands dropping to his sides.

"I've already mentioned our age difference."

"And I said it doesn't bother me."

"Well, it bothers me."

"Tell me why." He knew they'd come full circle, wondering if going 'round and 'round was Camilla's plan to discourage him. Sean refused to be thwarted.

"The biggest reason is I'm probably too old to have children."

"Would you like them?"

"Of course. I'd always envisioned a large family." She turned to face him. "What about you?"

He shrugged. "I never thought much about it."

"Now that we're talking about children, what would you say?"

"I come from a large family. It would seem logical for me to want several children, though it isn't something I worry about."

She offered a slow nod. "The odds are I won't be able to provide you with children." Pacing several feet away, she continued. "I spoke to a doctor in New York two years before leaving for Montana. Even then, he said the odds of having a healthy baby weren't good."

"We could seek other options."

"Such as?"

"You, more than most, understand the need for couples to adopt orphaned children. If marriage is where our relationship goes, we'll adopt."

Camilla had thought about adopting. She'd just never expected to meet a man open to the idea.

"When I'm fifty, you'll be turning forty. I'll be an

old woman while you'll be middle aged."

"Age is a number. There's no certainty of how any of us will handle aging. Back in California, there are any number of people in their sixties and seventies who are active. They raise cattle and farm animals, ride horses, and carry on the same as everyone else. Some even have the responsibility of raising their grandchildren. Wasn't it the same in New York?"

She shook her head. "The women I knew who were in their sixties were quite inactive. Thinking about it now, I don't know why. They did attend events and gave time to charities, but nothing compared to the women you describe."

"I may be asking you the wrong question." He walked to within a foot of her. "Do you see yourself staying here or returning to New York?"

"For now, I see myself staying." She walked to the sofa, sitting down. "Perhaps the lifestyle out here forces people to stay active as they age."

"It could also be your social standing made a difference."

"What do you mean?"

"You were in a higher class than most people. Servants did much of what you'll be doing if you choose to stay in Splendor. It's a hard life, Cam. People are forced to do for themselves. Living in the frontier changes people. You must be certain this is the life you want."

She liked the way he used the nickname Cole had

called her since they were children. "I understand Gabe and Lena Evans travel to New York every year. If I need rest, I could do the same."

A slow smile crossed his face on a chuckle. "Yes, you could. But that isn't what truly bothers you about a courtship, is it?"

Whirling away, she walked into the kitchen, picking up, then setting down the pot on the stove. Bracing her hands on the counter, she shook her head. "No."

"Tell me what else troubles you."

Closing her eyes, she didn't move from her spot in the kitchen. One minute, then two passed before her eyes opened and she turned to face him, her gaze unfocused.

"There was this man. As you might guess, Evan was six years younger than me. He was brilliant, a scholar of some note. Our families were close, our fathers best friends. We spent a great deal of time together before he proposed. We discussed the issue of our age difference, and like you, he said it didn't matter to him."

Releasing a breath, she blinked several times. "Evan accepted a teaching position at a well-respected college. Several months later, he requested we end our engagement." She chuckled without mirth. "Seems he'd compromised a girl who was employed as a clerk in his department. They married a week later." Her gaze bore into Sean's. "*One week later.* Within a month, it was quite obvious she was with child, perhaps three or four months along. He'd been seeing her for months before..." Her voice trailed off.

When she didn't continue, he closed the distance between them, taking her hands in his. "I'm not Evan. I'd never do anything which would knowingly cause you pain."

Staring down at their joined hands, she remained silent.

"Will you at least consider my request, Camilla?" He waited, until certain she wouldn't answer. "Camilla?"

"All right, Sean. I promise I'll give it serious thought."

Camilla dipped her pen into the inkwell and hovered over the blank paper on her desk. With a steady hand, she began to write.

My Dearest Theodore,

So much has happened since I last wrote you. Splendor is a town of excitement and adventure, though not without its share of troubles. Why, just in the last month, we had a foiled kidnapping attempt and a bank robbery right on our main street. But the townsfolk came together with courage and resilience to face the danger. Their determination gives me hope.

The landscape here is breathtaking, with

snowcapped mountains that take my breath away each morning. And there are the people. Rough around the edges but with hearts of gold. I've been volunteering at the orphanage, and those children bring me such joy. Their laughter lifts my spirits.

Of course, I know you'll worry for my safety, but I assure you I am fine. My spill from the horse last month gave me a fright, but I'm fully recovered now.

Theodore, I know you'll fret about me being out here alone, but I feel stronger than ever before. The wide open space has been good for my soul. I feel a confidence I've never known back east. This town has challenges, but it is a good place, filled with good people.

Now, I best finish. I know it's been too long since my last letter. I hope this finds you well. Please give my love to your beautiful family. I think of you often and can't wait to share more stories in person one day soon.

Yours faithfully,
Camilla

She set down her pen and scrutinized the letter. Satisfied she'd captured the essence of her experiences, she copied the contents into a separate letter for her other brother, Harrison.

Martha knocked lightly on the front door before letting herself into Camilla's house.

"Afternoon, Miss Camilla. I hope I'm not intruding."

"Not at all, Martha. Please, come in."

She sat down in the chair opposite Camilla's desk. "Writing more letters home?"

"Yes, just finishing up some notes to my brothers back east." She held up the letters. "I was telling them about life here in Splendor. All the recent goings-on, like the bank robbery and my little spill from the horse. And, of course, how much I've come to care for the people here."

Martha nodded, though her expression grew serious. "I don't mean to overstep, but are you sure it's wise to be telling your family every little thing that happens here? Those brothers of yours already thought this town was too wild for a lady before you came. Seems to me hearing about shootouts and such will only make them more inclined to think so."

She considered Martha's words, knowing the woman meant well. She didn't want to hide the truth from her brothers. This was her life now, and she wanted them to understand fully.

"I appreciate your concern, but I'd rather they know precisely what's going on. The good and the bad both. I'm not scared off easily, and I want them to realize this is the town I've chosen."

Martha nodded with reluctance. "I understand. I just hope the letters don't make them try to convince you to leave."

"They won't. This is my home now. No matter what they say."

The two spoke a while longer on town happenings, Camilla deciding not to mention Sean's request. When Martha left, she returned her attention to the letters. She folded and sealed them, determined for her brothers to know her experiences unvarnished. For better or worse, this was her life now. And she wouldn't change it for the world.

Camilla made her way to the post office, letters in hand. She nodded in greeting to folks she passed along Frontier Street, feeling a surge of fondness for this rugged town she now called home.

Stepping inside the telegraph and post office, she saw Bernie Griggs behind the counter, energy buzzing off him as he sorted through a stack of envelopes.

"Afternoon, Miss Camilla," Bernie greeted with a tip of his hat. "What can I do for you today?"

"I have two letters for my brothers back east." She handed them over. "I'd appreciate you getting them sent off quick as you can."

"Will do. New York…"

"That's right."

Bernie glanced at the addresses and set them aside. "I'll make sure they go out as soon as possible."

"Thank you, Bernie. Have a good rest of your day."

She strolled back outside, a lightness in her step. It would take a week for the letters to reach Theodore and Harrison, but she was eager for her brothers to understand this bold, spirited town and its people. And to understand her place among them.

Strolling down the street, she spotted Cole exiting the sheriff's office, Stetson in hand. Her brother's face lit up when he saw her.

"Afternoon, Cam. Care to join me for a bite at the boardinghouse?"

She laughed, thinking of Sean's use of her nickname. "I'd love to."

"I was thinking of Suzanne's hearty stew."

She tucked her arm through her brother's proffered one. "Stew sounds perfect."

The siblings made their way toward the boardinghouse, the noonday sun warm on their shoulders. Camilla breathed deep, savoring the sage-scented air.

Cole held open the boardinghouse door and ushered her inside. The interior was bright and cheery. ..and busy.

Suzanne looked up from wiping down a table, flashing them an engaging smile. "Hello, you two. Stew's hot and ready."

He led her over to a table near the front windows. Camilla settled into her chair, gazing out at the bustling street. Townsfolk went about their business, ladies with shopping parcels, men on horseback, children playing stickball in the side street. It was a heartening sight.

Suzanne took their orders, returning with two bowls of stew. She set them down, along with spoons and slices of warm bread.

"Thank you, Suzanne." Camilla tore off a chunk of bread before scooping up a mouthful of the thick beef stew.

He watched her, a thoughtful look on his face. "I wanted to ask...have you given more thought to what you'll do? Will you go back to New York?"

She paused mid-bite, staring down at her bowl, brow furrowed.

"I'm not certain," she admitted. "A large part of me wishes to stay, but..." She trailed off. Despite her excitement about a life in Splendor, the truth was, she felt torn. "I'm vacillating between this new life and my old world back east. Between independence and duty. Between my dreams and the family's expectations."

Cole reached over and squeezed her hand. "You've got time yet to decide. Just know Martha and I will support you, no matter what you choose."

Camilla offered him a grateful smile. She hoped when the time came, the choice would be clear. For now, all she could do was take things one day at a time.

Starting with finishing this delicious stew.

Chapter Sixteen

Camilla arrived at the orphanage several days later to a chorus of excited shouts and laughter, the smiling faces of children rushing to greet her. She wasted no time organizing games and activities, helping the little ones with their chores and lessons, bringing a sense of stability to their routine.

As she read to the children in the parlor, a knock sounded at the door. She opened it to find Deputy Morgan Wheeler, tipping his hat. "Ma'am. Is Mrs. Martha Santori available?"

Camilla showed Morgan inside and walked with him to Martha's office. He removed his hat, nodding at her. "Pardon the intrusion, Mrs. Santori. I wanted to offer my assistance with any repairs or heavy lifting needed."

Martha smiled. "That's very kind of you, Deputy. I'm sure we can find plenty for you to do." She knew his fondness for Amelia, the cook at the orphanage, was part of his motivation.

Morgan spent the afternoon fixing the creaky porch steps and chopping firewood, sneaking glances at Amelia when she passed by. Camilla enjoyed watching the way the two acted around each other, while keeping the children occupied with reading lessons and outdoor activities.

By supper time, the children were tuckered out. Camilla and Amelia tucked them into bed as Morgan rocked quietly in the parlor, working on a project of his own.

As the last child drifted off to sleep, he finished whittling the small owl figurine he planned to give Amelia. He slipped quietly from the room, finding her in the kitchen, washing dishes.

"Miss Newhall, I wanted to give you this, to thank you for the fine supper." He held out the owl.

Amelia's face lit up. She held it in her hand, admiring the craftmanship. "Why, it's beautiful. You've quite a talent, Deputy."

Their eyes met, and Morgan felt his heart squeeze. "It was my pleasure. I'll take any excuse to carve if it brings a smile to your face."

Amelia blushed, touched by his thoughtfulness. They talked softly as she finished her chores, the kitchen glowing in the lamp light. When finished, he bid her goodnight, joining Camilla for the ride back to town.

Sean arrived at Camilla's house a few days later, ponying her horse behind him. "It's a beautiful day for a ride around the countryside. Cole, Martha, and Dante will join us at the edge of town. They said to tell you their saddlebags are filled with food." He slipped to the ground, helping her mount.

They met up with the others, riding through wildflower meadows and hills dotted with pine, the wind tossing her hair. Laughter carried on the breeze as the five traded stories and jokes, falling into easy conversation.

When they stopped by a stream to rest, Camilla sighed. "I've not felt such freedom in years. I'm so glad all of you could come."

Cole grinned. "It's our pleasure. I enjoy seeing your spirits soar."

Martha nodded. "I'm so glad you organized this, Camilla. It's easy to take all this beauty for granted."

Remounting, they continued. As they approached a clearing, Dante's eyes grew wide.

"Father! Look at the horses." In the distance, a herd of horses grazed.

"Those are wild mustangs, Dante. Be real quiet and we'll watch them awhile."

The group quieted, their attention focused on the band of horses. After a time, the leader, a chestnut stallion, reared up and ran. The rest of the herd followed after him.

"This is a good place to eat lunch," Sean suggested.

"Suits me." Cole dismounted, helping Martha down before untying the saddlebags holding the food.

The women spread out two large blankets, setting out food while Sean, Cole, and Dante walked the area.

"This is a beautiful spot, Camilla." Martha looked around, taking a deep breath of the cool mountain air. "Between his work in town and mine at the orphanage, it's hard for Cole, Dante, and me to get away as a family. This is perfect."

Finishing the food the women set out, the four adults relaxed. Dante jumped up, running around the meadow to see what the meadow held. Butterflies, birds, rabbits—everything caught his attention.

"Dante sure has taken to Montana. I wasn't certain he would." Camilla tucked her feet underneath her, watching her nephew search for whatever he could find. He'd lived with her in New York before Cole took him west.

"Father!" Dante ran back to the adults, his face bright with excitement.

Cole smiled at his antics. "What is it?"

"We should name this place Mustang Meadow. Because of the horses. Is that all right?"

"Fine with me."

"Great!" Dante took off again, this time toward the copse of trees.

"He never slows down." Martha smiled, watching him disappear into the brush. "Dante loves everything. He's such a joy."

Just then, a scream came from where Dante had disappeared. Jumping up, Cole ran toward the last spot they'd seen him, Sean right behind him. As they arrived at the edge of the meadow, Dante ran to Cole.

"I saw a wolf. A big one." He pointed behind him. "It's on the other side of the stream."

Cole gripped his shoulders. "Dante, I want you to calm down. We're going back to the women, pack up, and leave. Do not run or yell. We'll do this as quietly as we can. You stick right by me, understand?"

"Yes, sir."

"All right then."

Reaching the women, Cole explained what Dante had seen. "Pack up as quick as possible. Limit the noise. We need to leave as soon as the saddlebags are tied."

As he spoke, Dante continued to glance behind him. He searched the trees and bushes for any sign of the wolf. Helping fold one of the blankets, he stilled as a low, guttural growl emanated from the brush several yards behind him. Dante's eyes grew wide with fear.

Hearing the ominous sounds, Cole and Sean drew their pistols and scanned the area. Among the tangled branches, they spotted the dark form of a wolf.

"Dante, mount up, now," Sean said under his breath.

The boy scrambled back to his horse, swinging up into the saddle with the ease of a seasoned rider. His horse danced around, whinnying in fright.

Cole and Sean kept their pistols aimed at the wolf while the women mounted their horses.

"Martha, Cam, and Dante. Head out. Sean and I will be right behind you."

The three didn't hesitate to walk their horses several paces before kicking them into a trot.

"Let's move out, Sean."

Both mounted, following the others. With a final glance back at the wolf, the group urged their horses into a brisk lope, eager to put distance between themselves and the predator.

Dante couldn't help slowing enough to look behind him once more before catching up with the others. His heart pounded with exhilaration as they raced back toward home and safety.

The group rode into Splendor as the sun disappeared below the horizon, casting the town in a darkening glow. Dismounting in front of the livery, Cole clasped Dante on the shoulder.

"You did good today, son. You stayed calm, even when the wolf was so close."

Dante beamed, delighted at his father's praise.

Camilla and Sean lingered near their horses. Their eyes met and held for a moment. There was so much Sean wanted to say, but now wasn't the time.

"I'll walk you home."

"All right." She slipped her arm through his, waving to the others as they left.

Sean said little as they walked through the almost deserted streets. Camilla was so different from most women he'd met. She was also highly intelligent, kind, yet with a bold spirit and streak of independence uncommon in most people—man or woman.. He hoped she'd soon give him an answer about courting her.

"I hope I haven't been too forward, but I confess my feelings for you have grown these past weeks."

She met his gaze, her heart fluttering. "Truthfully, Sean, I've spent a good deal of time thinking about your request. I'm quite fond of you. My concern about the age difference hasn't changed. I don't want you to feel trapped as we get older."

He turned to face her. "If our relationship progresses as I hope, you'll never have to worry about me feeling trapped."

"Well, perhaps we can take it slow, make certain you realize what you're getting yourself into."

Sean's face lit up. "Then you'll allow me to formally court you?"

Camilla smiled. "I believe I will."

Sean whooped while Camilla laughed. He pulled her closer, his hands lingering on her waist.

"Thank you for making me the happiest man in Montana."

As they said goodnight, Sean pressed a kiss against her lips.

She watched him walk away, hugging herself around the waist as excitement for what was to come settled over her.

The next day, Camilla visited the orphanage again, eager to share her happy news with Martha. The children's joyful shouts surrounded her as she entered.

"Good morning," she called out, embracing each child.

Martha gave her a knowing look. "I take it Sean finally worked up the nerve to court you properly?"

Camilla laughed. "Your intuition is correct, as always. I confess I'm quite taken with him."

The children gathered around her, ending the conversation with Martha. Clamoring to hear about her trail ride adventure, they wouldn't stop chattering until she took a seat in the parlor. The boys and girls dropped onto the rug around her. Martha took a chair nearby. She indulged their curiosity, describing the majestic mustangs and peaceful meadow they discovered.

"My nephew named it Mustang Meadow, in honor of the beautiful wild horses we saw there."

The children murmured excitedly at her story. Young Robbie spoke up. "I wanna see the mustangs! Can we go there, Miss Camilla?"

She ruffled his hair. "Perhaps. Someday, I'll organize an outing for all of you to visit. Would you like that?"

The children cheered in response.

"Let me finish telling you the rest." When she got

to the part about the wolf, their eyes grew huge.

"A real wolf?"

Two older brothers stood off to the side, snickering. She guessed spotting a wolf wasn't an uncommon event in their lives. Until he'd died, they'd been raised by their father. One of the brothers enjoyed sharing stories of their father's adventures.

Camilla continued the tale, embellishing some details to add to the drama and excitement. By the end, the children were enthralled, begging for more adventures.

"Just one more story, Miss Santori," one young boy begged.

Before she could respond, Deputy Morgan Wheeler ambled in, touching the brim of his hat toward Camilla and Martha. "Morning, ladies. I'm here to fix the loose step on your back porch."

Martha stood. "That's very kind of you, Deputy. If you don't mind, please head back to the kitchen. Amelia will be glad to show you the issues we're having. We have lemonade for when you've finished."

Morgan nodded, flashing a grin at her. "Much obliged, ma'am."

As he headed outside, Camilla thought of the shy smiles between Morgan and Amelia. She made a mental note to ask Martha about her suspicions.

For now, Camilla focused her attention on the children, leading them in songs and reading stories aloud. Their joyous laughter echoed through the rooms.

Chapter Seventeen

Harrison leaned back in his seat and gazed out the train window, the landscape passing by in a blur. His younger brother, Theodore, sat across from him, frowning at the telegram in his hand.

"I still can't believe Camilla wants to stay in a grimy little frontier town," Theodore said. "Splendor sounds wholly unfit for a woman of her standing."

"Yes, it's troubling, especially after she described the attempted kidnapping." Harrison shook his head. "Splendor is no place for our sister. She belongs back in New York with her family."

Theodore refolded the telegram. "Father would never have allowed this. He would've marched right out to Montana and dragged Camilla back himself if he were still alive."

"Which is exactly why we're going. We must talk some sense into her and bring her home where she belongs." Harrison checked his pocket watch, anxiety creeping into his voice. "This blasted train can't move fast enough. I knew we should've taken the northern route."

Theodore smirked. "There is no northern route, Harry. Another reason for avoiding travel to this part of the country."

Right on cue, the train began to slow as it pulled into the next station. The brothers exchanged exasperated looks.

"Another stop? This is the third one today." Theodore looked out the window, glaring at the platform outside. "Absolutely unacceptable. We'll never reach Splendor at this rate."

Theodore stood to pace the narrow train car.

"Try to be patient," Harrison said as his brother passed by him for the third time. "I'm as frustrated as you are, but getting angry won't speed this train along."

"I know you're right, and we both saw the schedule providing all the stops. Her telegram has me bothered beyond reason." Theodore sat back down, his gaze fixed on the scenery outside.

After what seemed an eternity, the train lurched forward, continuing its laborious journey west. The Rocky Mountain peaks loomed closer, both beautiful and menacing.

Somewhere beyond those mountains lay the tiny town of Splendor—and their unpredictable sister, Camilla.

After three long days on the train, Harrison and Theodore arrived in Cheyenne, Wyoming, exhausted and anxious. Both knew their journey wasn't over yet.

The brothers secured seats on the next stagecoach

departing for Big Pine, the territorial capital. Settling into the cramped coach, both were eager to complete this leg of the trip.

The stage travelled over the rough terrain, mountain passes, and through Indian territory without delay. They'd almost made it when fate interfered.

Just as they approached the outskirts of Big Pine, there was a sudden, loud cracking sound. The coach tilted violently to one side as the front wheel splintered.

"Confound it!" Theodore exploded, bracing himself against the side of the coach.

The driver brought the damaged coach to a jolting halt. After inspecting the broken wheel, he regretfully informed the passengers it could take at least two days for a replacement to be built and installed.

Theodore let out a string of ungentlemanly phrases, but there was nothing to be done except wait in Big Pine. Two more precious days lost before they could confront Camilla.

They caught some good luck before sunrise the following morning. The blacksmith had worked all night, building a new wheel. By six o'clock, the stage was back on the trail to Splendor.

Camilla, Martha Santori, and Lena Evans sat at a table in the Eagle's Nest restaurant. Ignoring other diners and the elegant surroundings, the women carried on an animated conversation about the most recent fundraising plans for the orphanage. Camilla's eyes shone with enthusiasm as she described some new ideas to engage the local community.

"Oh, Lena, if we could get a few more families to sponsor a child, it would ease our expenses considerably. I know money is tight, but surely we can appeal to people's generosity."

Lena nodded. "Perhaps a social event with a raffle? Maybe the church women could be persuaded to donate quilts, or canned goods. Everyone loves Ruth Paige's fruit preserves. Stores in town might be willing to provide items from their shelves for the raffle."

Lena tapped a finger against her lips, eyes going wide on a thought. "You two haven't met him because he's been in Europe. Baron Ernst Wolfgang Klaussner, and his son, Johann, are returning within the week from a two-year trip. Johann must be seventeen by now. Anyway, Klaussner is a generous man, and he is a good friend of Walter Evans, Gabe's father. I'll speak with Walter about approaching Klaussner."

"Both are wonderful ideas." Martha turned toward her sister-in-law. "We'll make it happen, Camilla. If anyone can inspire contributions, it's the women in this town."

Camilla was about to respond when she caught sight of two familiar figures entering the restaurant. Her mouth fell open in surprise as she recognized her brothers, Harrison and Theodore.

The men's eyes scanned the room until they spotted Camilla. Relief washed over their tired faces.

"Camilla! Thank heavens you're all right." Harrison grasped her hands in greeting, bending down to kiss her cheek.

Theodore wore a deep frown. "We've come to bring you back to New York. This frontier life is far too dangerous for you."

Camilla's shock turned to irritation. Clearly, her letters had done nothing to ease their misplaced worries. She opened her mouth to protest, but Martha beat her to it.

"You must be Camilla's brothers. I'm Martha Santori, Cole's wife and your sister-in-law." She extended her hand. "Welcome to Splendor."

The brothers gaped at Martha in utter shock. This refined, aristocratic looking woman living out west? It was unthinkable.

Theodore recovered first. "A pleasure to meet you." He grasped her extended hand before Harrison did the same.

An awkward tension descended on the group. The contrasting sensibilities of east versus west were on full display. As the easterners were about to learn, Camilla had no intention of leaving. Splendor was her home now.

She took a deep breath to calm her rising irritation. This conversation would require delicacy and tact.

"Harrison, Theodore, why don't we continue this discussion at my house? It's a five minute walk."

The brothers exchanged a look. "Of course," Harrison agreed. He was anxious to get her alone so they could make her see reason.

She bid Lena and Martha a quick goodbye before leading her brothers outside. They walked in tense silence along the rutted streets.

When they stepped inside her cozy home, the brothers looked around in dismay.

"You actually live here?" Theodore asked incredulously.

Camilla bristled at his tone. "Yes, I do. And I happen to love it."

Harrison chose his response carefully. "But it's so...small, and, well...rustic."

She whirled around to face them. "I know you're concerned for my well-being, and I'm grateful you've come all this way to check on me. But Splendor is my home now. I'm quite happy here."

Theodore shook his head angrily. "Happy? Bandits accosted you in the street! This town is dangerous, especially for a woman alone."

"I can take care of myself just fine. Why, many of the women in town have been taking lessons on how to properly fire a gun."

"A gun! Are you out of your mind? Tell her how ridiculous this sounds, Harrison."

The oldest of the two brothers shook his head, not

ready to respond.

"And I'm not alone. I have wonderful friends here, including Lena and our sister-in-law, Martha. And let's not forget our brother, Cole, is a deputy sheriff in town."

Harrison took her hands in his. "Please, sister. Be sensible and come home with us. We've been sick with worry."

She set her jaw. "Understand, Harry. I've made my choice. I'm staying."

The brothers stared at her in frustrated disbelief. How could she be so stubborn?

Just then, a knock sounded at the door. Camilla opened it to find Sean standing on her porch.

"Hello, Camilla. I heard your brothers were in town." Sean took in the scene before him. He hesitated in the doorway, sensing the tension in the room.

"Am I interrupting something?"

"No, not at all. Come in. Let me introduce you to my brothers, Harrison and Theodore Santori. And this is Sean MacLaren. He's the area veterinarian."

The brothers nodded curtly.

"To what do we owe the pleasure?" Theodore's icy demeanor wasn't lost on Sean.

He squared his shoulders. "I just wanted to stop by and assure you, gentlemen, your sister is safe here in Splendor. We may be a small town, but we take care of our own."

Harrison scoffed. "Clearly not, if she was nearly

kidnapped right on your streets."

"It was an isolated incident, I can promise you," Sean replied.

"My brothers seem to think Splendor is far too dangerous for a woman.”

Sean offered a sympathetic smile. "With all due respect, your sister has proven herself quite capable here. She's become a valued member of this community."

"Be that as it may, our family expects her to return to New York at once," Theodore said.

Camilla's eyes flashed. "My siblings don’t get to decide my fate."

"Please try to understand..."

"I understand perfectly, Harry. You still see me as a helpless female in need of your protection. But I don't need it anymore. After all, I am the oldest. I can decide my own future."

The brothers fell silent, struggling to grasp her defiant independence.

Sean’s voice softened. "Change is difficult. But living in the frontier has been good for Camilla. Perhaps in time, you'll see Splendor as her home...and yours as well."

The brothers exchanged doubtful glances. Camilla took a deep breath.

"Why don't we all sit down to a nice supper tonight and continue this conversation? I'm sure we can find some common ground."

After a moment of indecision, Harrison and Theodore agreed.

"Where are you staying?" Sean asked.

Harrison answered. "The St. James hotel."

"Best hotel in the western territory. Why don't we eat at their restaurant, Eagle's Nest?"

Theodore shot a look at his brother, who nodded. "All right. Shall we say seven?"

"Seven is fine." Camilla kissed each brother on his cheek. "And...thank you."

Chapter Eighteen

The Eagle's Nest restaurant was bustling with patrons when Sean MacLaren and Camilla Santori arrived for their dinner engagement. Theodore and Harrison were already seated at a quiet table in the back, perusing the menu while waiting for the couple's arrival.

"Good evening, gentlemen." Sean greeted them as he and Camilla approached the table.

Theodore stood to pull out Camilla's chair. "You look wonderful, as always."

"Thank you, Teddy. You selected a perfect spot to watch the comings and goings." Camilla offered a polite smile as she took her seat.

Harrison gave Sean a firm handshake. "Dr. MacLaren, thank you for joining us this evening."

"Please, call me Sean." He took his place next to Camilla.

A waiter arrived to take drink orders. As he departed, the foursome made pleasant small talk about the weather and recent town events. Beneath the civil veneer, tension simmered. Theodore and Harrison were determined to make their sister second-guess her decision to remain in Splendor. As Sean sensed the brothers' underlying motives, his guard raised in protection of the woman he cared about.

Theodore took a sip of whiskey before speaking. "So, Camilla, what made you decide to stay on in Splendor? Last we spoke, you planned to return to New York after a brief holiday."

Camilla straightened in her chair. "As you know, my time here has been enlightening. I've found purpose in supporting the orphanage, and helping out in the community."

"Is small town life enough for someone of your station?" Harrison asked pointedly.

Sean bristled at the insulting implication, but held his tongue.

Camilla's eyes flashed. "I don't see it as limiting in the least. Rather, it's been liberating to step outside of societal constraints and expectations."

Theodore leaned forward, his gaze intense. "And what of your associations? Are you certain they meet your new...standards?"

The insinuation was clear. Sean gripped his glass tightly, muscles taut. He would not let these pompous men disparage him.

"I'm more than satisfied with the company I've found here," Camilla replied. "Now, tell me, when does construction begin on the new hotel you're building in New York?"

With that, the conversation moved to safer topics. But the undercurrent of tension lingered, unresolved.

Sean tried to steer the conversation toward neutral

topics as the main course arrived. Waiting for Camilla to take a bite of her meal, he picked up his fork.

"The beef stew looks delicious."

Ignoring Sean, Theodore and Harrison continued to press Camilla.

"You can't truly wish to spend your days in this dirty backwater hovel." Theodore's amused tone grated on Sean. "What of society, culture, intellectual pursuits?"

Harrison joined in. "And the company of proper gentlemen, rather than..." He trailed off, but his meaning was obvious as he glanced at Sean.

Jaw clenched, he held back an angry retort.

Camilla's eyes blazed. "I'll thank you not to disparage my choices. I find Splendor charming, not lacking. And I'm rather fond of the *company*."

She reached over and squeezed Sean's hand. He felt a rush of gratitude and affection.

To his dismay, Theodore and Harrison were relentless. As the meal progressed, their not so subtle barbs became outright insults aimed at Sean.

With each callous remark, his temper rose. The time had come to take a stand.

Taking a deep breath, he worked to keep his voice steady.

"Gentlemen, I understand your concern for your sister's well-being. But there's no call for rudeness. I may not have a fancy pedigree, but I work hard, and care deeply for Camilla."

She gave him an encouraging smile. Emboldened, he continued.

"As for Splendor, you're right about it lacking opera houses or soirees. The people more than make up for those omissions. They're kind and true. Camilla will be surrounded by community, not stifling social expectations, judgmental relatives, or friends who'd desert her in the most desperate times."

He looked at Camilla, his eyes shining with sincerity. "This town nurtures the soul in a way high society never could."

Theodore scoffed. "Don't pretend you can provide the comfortable life she's accustomed to."

Anger flared in Sean. "Money isn't everything. We'll build a good life together."

Harrison's laugh held no warmth. "You're hardly worthy of an esteemed family like the Santoris."

"How dare you!" Camilla burst out. "Sean is the most honorable man I know. You insult me with your contempt." She threw her napkin down and stood. "I'm ashamed to call you brothers."

With that, she stormed out, leaving the men stunned in her wake.

Though shaken by her abrupt exit, Sean felt an intense stirring of emotion at her staunch defense.

After a taut moment, Sean tossed his napkin down, shot a contemptuous glance at Harrison and Theodore, before following Camilla.

Hurrying out of the restaurant, Sean scanned the

dark street for any sign of her. He spotted a slender form in front of the Splendor Emporium's window. He rushed to catch up.

"Camilla..."

She turned, eyes glistening with angry tears. Sean's heart ached at her distress.

"I'm so sorry about my brothers. Their arrogance and disdain are inexcusable."

"You have nothing to apologize for. I'm just relieved you stood up for yourself. And...for me."

"Of course. You're the best man I've ever known." She sighed. "I just wish my brothers could see that."

Sean covered her hand with his own. "It doesn't matter what they think. What does matter is what we feel for each other."

"You always know exactly what to say." She exhaled a shaky breath, emotions still raw. "Would you be interested in walking me home?"

Sean nodded, relieved she didn't ask him to accompany her back into the restaurant. He leaned down to kiss her before offering his arm. "I'd be honored."

The next morning, Cole Santori strode purposefully into the Eagle's Nest, where his brothers were having breakfast. Harrison and Theodore looked up in surprise as Cole approached their table.

"Good morning, Cole." Harrison motioned for him to sit down.

Cole's expression was stern. "I think you know why I'm here. Let's talk upstairs."

The brothers exchanged an uneasy glance but rose without objection. In Theodore's room, Cole crossed his arms and faced them.

"I want an explanation for what I've been hearing this morning. What in blazes were you thinking last night?"

Theodore bristled. "Now see here, Cole, that's none of your—"

"The heck it isn't," Cole interrupted. "You insulted and belittled our sister, your own flesh and blood. And Sean, one of the most upstanding men in town. All because they don't fit your arrogant notions of propriety."

Harrison held up a hand in a cautious gesture. "Perhaps we were...overzealous. But we only want what's best for Camilla."

Cole scoffed. "Clearly, you don't know what that is. She's happy here, happier than she's been her whole life. And you're too self-absorbed to see it."

Theodore looked affronted, but Harrison had the grace to appear contrite.

Cole pressed on. "You're going to apologize to both of them. Grovel, for all I care. Make this right, or you'll regret it."

His brothers exchanged another look as Cole

stormed from the room, realization dawning. They'd damaged something precious. With grudging resolve, they nodded.

Theodore and Harrison left the hotel in somber silence, both lost in thought as they made their way along the boardwalk. Though neither wanted to admit it aloud, Cole's words had struck a chord. In their eagerness to prove Camilla was making a mistake, they'd insulted Sean and wounded her deeply.

Theodore was the first to break the heavy quiet. "I fear we've made a right mess of things, old boy."

Harrison nodded, his expression grim. "Quite. We should have trusted Camilla's judgment instead of assuming we knew best."

"And that Sean fellow. I confess we may have misjudged him. He seems an honorable man, if a bit rough around the edges."

As they made a full circle back to the hotel, Harrison clasped his brother's shoulder. "We'll make this right. She'll surely forgive us once she knows our hearts were in the right place."

"I do hope so. I should hate to lose my favorite sister over a bout of foolish pride."

"As would I." Harrison smiled. "Have faith. The Santori clan is not so easily broken."

With lifted spirits and contrite hearts, the brothers entered the hotel to pen earnest apologies to Camilla and Sean, hoping to repair the bonds of family they had so thoughtlessly frayed.

Within the hour, Theodore and Harrison made their way to Camilla's house. As they approached, she appeared through the front window, arms crossed, watching them. Dropping her arms, she opened the door to usher them inside, leaving the front door open.

"Good morning, Camilla," Harrison said.

Camilla looked at them, her expression guarded. "To what do I owe the pleasure?"

Theordore shoved his hands into the pockets of his trousers and cleared his throat. "We've come to apologize in person for our appalling behavior last night. You didn't deserve any of it."

After a long moment, she made her decision. "I accept your apology. But it will take time to reclaim my trust."

Harrison nodded. "Of course. Thank you for giving us the chance."

The sounds of a horse approaching caught their attention. Sean reined up in front of her house, spotting the three through the open door. Dismounting, he approached with a wary expression. His attention locked on Camilla.

"Everything all right here?"

"Yes. My brothers came to make amends."

"Is that so?"

Theodore took a deep breath as he prepared to

broach the next difficult topic.

"There's one more thing we must do to make this right," Theodore said. "Sean, we owe you an apology as well for the deplorable way we spoke of you last night. We had no call to insult your profession or question your intentions. We sincerely regret the offense we caused you." He extended his hand. "We hope you can forgive us."

Sean considered him for a moment before accepting his hand, then Harrison's. "Apology accepted," he said finally. "Let's move forward from here."

Camilla smiled at both of her brothers. "I'm glad we could have this talk. It means a lot to me that you want to make things right."

Cole Santori strode up her porch. He paused when he saw the group gathered inside.

"Everything all right in here?"

"Yes, everything is fine," Camilla said. "Theodore and Harrison were just apologizing for their boorish behavior last night."

Cole nodded, a hint of a smile touching his lips. "Good to hear." He looked at Theodore and Harrison. "Why don't you and Sean show them the town? When you're finished, we can meet at the boardinghouse restaurant for lunch."

Chapter Nineteen

The streets of Splendor bustled with activity as Camilla, Sean, Harrison, and Theodore made their way through town. Camilla's face lit up as she introduced the brothers to various shop owners and town leaders encountered along their stroll.

"Sitting on the bench up ahead is Enoch Weaver," she said. "Cole told me he came to Splendor from back east, where he was a respected attorney. Enoch sometimes helps the sheriff and his deputies identify outlaws."

"He doesn't appear as a man who could help the sheriff." Harrison's gaze narrowed on the man's shabby appearance.

Camilla nodded. "The exact point. People talk freely around him, assuming he's passed out or sleeping."

Harrison tipped his hat while Theodore offered a greeting. "Good day to you, sir."

Enoch returned the gestures with a knowing smile.

Continuing down the crowded boardwalk, Camilla regaled them with stories of the town and its inhabitants.

"It hasn't always been easy here. I've discovered

these folks are a resilient bunch. Why, when the cattle fever hit a few years back and wiped out half the herds, I heard no one complained or packed up and left. Folks tightened their belts and got through it together."

Sean agreed. "This town has weathered its share of storms over the years. Each time, the community always rallies. Their determination is inspiring."

Camilla's eyes shone with pride. "Compared to New York City, Splendor is a relatively young town, but it has more heart and grit than cities ten times its size."

The group soon arrived at the general store, its windows filled with a wide variety of wares. As they stepped inside, Camilla recognized two men she wanted her brothers to meet.

"Dax, Luke, meet my brothers visiting from New York, Theodore and Harrison."

The men shook hands firmly as Sean spoke up. "Dax and Luke Pelletier own Redemption's Edge ranch north of town. I understand it's the largest cattle and horse operation in western Montana."

Dax spoke in his commanding southern drawl. "Luke and I have been running cattle and horses since not long after the war. Ranching plays a huge part in this community's success."

As they discussed recent developments, such as a possible railway spur and cattle prices, it became clear the Pelletier brothers' ranching operation was indispensable to local commerce.

After several more minutes of stimulating

conversation, the group said their goodbyes before continuing down the boardwalk.

"Quite a fascinating operation those two have going," Theodore remarked.

"Cattle ranchers appear to play a vital role out here," Harrison agreed.

"They do," Sean said. "Ranchers were the first pioneers to settle this land. Everything was built on the backs of their hard work and sacrifice."

The group soon arrived at a large livery stable and blacksmith shop. The ringing of a hammer on anvil could be heard from within.

Stepping inside, they were greeted by Noah Brandt. After quick introductions, he welcomed the brothers to town.

"Splendor's growing every day by people searching for a new life and better opportunities," Noah explained. "So far this year, my men have built ten new houses and four buildings. I guarantee more people are on their way."

Theodore offered a thoughtful nod. "Are you providing housing for all these newcomers?"

Noah chuckled. "For some. My wife and I own a majority of the houses and buildings in town."

"Sean and I both rent our houses from Noah," Camilla said.

As Noah and the brothers discussed business prospects and opportunities in the bustling town, it was clear Splendor's future looked bright. The people were hopeful, the spirit determined. This settlement on the Montana frontier was thriving thanks to unified effort, vision, and grit.

Soon enough, their tour continued down Frontier Street. The boardinghouse restaurant came into view, a quaint clapboard building with flower boxes in the windows. Stepping inside, they were greeted by Suzanne Barnett.

"So wonderful to meet Camilla's brothers," Suzanne exclaimed as Cole appeared beside them. She showed them to a table near the front window, the delicious fragrance of home cooking made their mouths water.

As they sat down to lunch, conversation turned to the Santori family back east. Though Splendor was far from New York, its pioneer spirit had left an enduring impression on Harrison and Theodore.

As their lunch came to an end, the group made their way outside. Theodore and Harrison announced they'd be catching the afternoon stagecoach to begin their journey back to New York.

"Thank you for the warm welcome you've shown us here in Splendor." Theodore shook Sean's hand. "It's been, well...enlightening, learning about Camilla's new life. And meeting you."

Harrison clasped Sean's outstretched hand. "I

agree, this has been a learning experience. Perhaps we should arrange a longer visit in the future. And bring our families."

Camilla's face lit up at the prospect. "Oh, yes, you simply must. There's still so much more for you to see."

Cole agreed. "We'd love to have you back anytime. Stay as long as you'd like."

"Well, safe travels." She forced a smile, swiping an errant tear from the corner of her eye. "We'll be awaiting your next visit. Splendor will always be open to you."

After a round of farewell hugs, Theodore and Harrison climbed aboard the stagecoach. As it rumbled out of sight, Camilla felt a touch of sadness. Sean squeezed her hand in a gesture of comfort and support.

"I know you wanted them to stay longer," he said softly. "It was a good first step that they came at all. This visit reopened the door between you."

Camilla nodded, blinking back tears. "You're right. I'm thankful for the time we had."

Cole put a reassuring hand on his sister's shoulder. "They'll be back, I'm sure of it. We made progress in educating our stodgy brothers."

"So true." Camilla chuckled. She linked her arm through Sean's. "Come, let's walk for a bit."

"I'm on my way back to the jail." Cole kissed his sister's cheek, shook Sean's hand, then crossed the street for the short walk to the sheriff's office.

As they watched Cole walk along the boardwalk,

another deputy ran up to him, arms motioning across the street as they spoke. The two deputies dodged horses and wagons as they crossed the street to enter Finn's saloon.

"I wonder what happened?" Sean quickened their pace.

Approaching the saloon, they heard raised voices and shouts coming from inside. A small crowd had gathered, looking on with anxious expressions. The sound of shattering glass made Camilla jump.

Sean's jaw tightened. "Stay back, I'll see if I can help Cole get this under control."

He moved into the chaotic scene. Camilla wrung her hands, pulse racing. After the calm of Theodore and Harrison's visit, the eruption of violence was a harsh awakening.

Camilla paced outside the saloon as the sounds of the brawl continued. She flinched as a bottle shattered against the doorframe.

"We should get you to safety, it's too dangerous here."

She hadn't noticed Deputy Cash Coulter standing beside her.

"I'm not leaving until I know Sean is all right."

When the saloon doors burst open, a bruised, bloodied miner came stumbling out, landing at her feet. Before Camilla could react, the man grabbed her leg in a rough grip.

Cash leapt forward to intervene. Two other

brawlers burst from the saloon, knocking into him. Camilla spotted the man reaching for his gun.

"Cash!" She stomped her heel down on her assailant's foot, wrenching herself free when he yowled in pain.

Whirling, she saw another miner reach for his six-shooter. Cash spun around, his fist connecting with the man's chin. He crumpled with a grunt.

Breathing hard, Camilla seized a fallen weapon, leveling it at the miners. "That's enough. All of you stop this instant or I'll start shooting."

The men froze at the steely determination in her voice. Cash stepped away from the scuffle, a grin spreading across his face.

Cole emerged from the saloon, dragging two bloodied men by their collars. Right behind him was Sean, sporting a split lip but otherwise unharmed.

Camilla lowered the pistol, her heart pounding as she took in the aftermath of the brawl. Shattered glass littered the wooden boardwalk. Crumpled forms of unconscious men lay strewn about, remnants of their drunken dispute.

Cole deposited the two men he'd hauled from the saloon next to the others. He gave Camilla a nod of gratitude as Sean came to stand beside her.

"Quite a mess." Sean gingerly touched his swollen lip.

Camilla nodded, but her unease remained.

Chapter Twenty

The dark clouds gathered on the horizon, swollen with rain. To the north, the river churned, its waters rising as the snowmelt from the mountains swelled its banks. Already the muddy torrent lapped at the foundations of the buildings lining Frontier Street. At Redemption's Edge ranch, most of the corrals and barns were flooded with close to a foot of water.

Dax Pelletier stood on the porch of the ranch house, his jaw set as he surveyed the damage. The floodwaters tore at the land he and his brother had poured years into building. He saw no sign the water had started to recede. Instead, the flood rose at a ferocious pace. Beside him, Luke stared in disbelief. They'd shored buildings up as best as they could, but their efforts were no match for the surging water.

"It's bad, Dax. Once it recedes, we'll rebuild. A raging river isn't going to run us out of business."

Dax nodded, though his eyes were grim. "It might if this blasted rain keeps up. We need to get the stock to high ground before the water takes them."

As if declaring a battle, the clouds opened up, unleashing a deluge of Biblical proportions. Luke and Dax scrambled to ready the horses and round up their cattle. The water rose faster than they could react, swallowing the lower pastures while surging toward outbuildings.

Within minutes, the current had grabbed two smaller sheds, wrenching them from their foundations and smashing them against trees and rocks farther downstream. The larger barns groaned under the pressure, boards splitting and nails shrieking as they loosened. For now, the barns held.

The brothers could do nothing except watch helplessly as the relentless tide destroyed in minutes what had taken years to build. Dax's hands clenched into fists, knuckles white as he watched the continued destruction.

The raging waters surged over the banks of Wildfire Creek, spilling onto the lower pastures of the ranch. Helpless animals struggled against the current, their terrified cries rising above the roar of the flood.

Young calves were ripped from their mother's sides, bleating frantically as they were dragged downstream. Horses fought to keep their heads above water, paddling furiously. Most managed to make it to higher ground, but others weren't so lucky.

From atop a hill overlooking the devastation at Redemption's Edge, Morgan Wheeler and deputies, Jonas Taylor and Tucker Nolan, surveyed the tragic scene below them. Gabe Evans had made a good decision, ordering them to assess the damage north of town. Their horses shifted uneasily, sensing the deputies' grim mood.

"We'd best get back to town, see how bad the flooding is there. We have to notify Gabe of what we've seen." Morgan wheeled his horse around. The others followed, somber expressions on their faces. They'd seen floods before, but never one this vicious or deadly.

Riding toward Splendor, Morgan couldn't help but feel a pang of grief for the poor creatures taken by the raging waters. But there would be time enough for mourning later. Right now, the living needed their help, including the children at the orphanage. With a deep breath, Morgan steeled himself for whatever they would find when they reached town.

Morgan and the other deputies arrived in Splendor to find the water threatening the edges of the boardwalk. Several buildings, those not raised much above the dirt streets, threatened collapse, while debris cluttered the town. Morgan rushed into the jail to find it empty.

Sloshing through the building water, he joined Tucker and Jonas. "No one's inside." Jumping off the edge of the boardwalk, he mounted his horse. "I have to ride to the orphanage."

"We're going with you," Jonas said.

As they rode toward the orphans home, Morgan spotted Amelia Newhall struggling to drive a wagon loaded with supplies out of a deep, water-filled hole.

"Here, let me help you." Morgan dismounted his horse, tossing the reins to Tucker before climbing onto the wagon seat next to her.

Amelia gave him a grateful smile. "Thank you. We're trying to get supplies to higher ground before the water ruins everything. Rose and Martha are working with Cole to get the children away from the flooding."

Jonas grabbed the harness of one horse, tugging it as Morgan slapped the reins. At first, the wagon didn't budge from the sticky mud. It took several tries before they succeeded.

Morgan guided the wagon up the hill, not allowing the wagon to venture off the narrow trail.

"How are you holding up?"

"Soaked clear through." She tugged her ridiculous cotton hat further down on her head. "As well as can be expected under the circumstances. I just hope we can get all the children to safety. The younger ones are so frightened."

He gave her the best reassuring look he could muster. "We'll make sure they stay safe. Jonas, Tucker, and I will escort you out of here soon."

Amelia placed her hand over his, eyes glistening. "You're a good man, Morgan Wheeler. I'm glad you're here."

His pulse quickened at her touch. He cleared his throat, glancing over his shoulder at the tarp covering the supplies. "Do you plan to leave the wagon at the top of the hill?"

"Until the rain stops and the flood recedes. Our most pressing issue is where to take the children. I'd planned to walk back and help the others keep everyone together."

"There's an old cabin not far from here, Amelia. It isn't in great condition. We can help get the children to it."

"It has to be better than anywhere else we could take them."

She nodded, her stomach roiling with worry.

He noticed her concern, fear for the children. It stirred something within him, though he couldn't define what. All he knew was he would do everything possible to protect Amelia and the children.

Sean and Camilla worked without rest as the floodwaters rose, focused on saving as many lives as possible. Though exhausted, they pushed on.

He led a group of men to a stranded family perched on their roof. Their house had been built in a low spot, which had turned into a deep pond as the rain continued.

"Hang tight, we're coming for you!"

The frigid water soaked him to the bone, the raging current slowed his progress. Sean and the others kept wading forward. Reaching the house, he helped lower the family, one at a time, into a canoe Noah had stored behind the livery.

Camilla spotted an elderly man clinging weakly to a tree branch. Without hesitation, she waded into the swirling rapids. Sean's heart clenched as the strong current stifled her movements. He surged in after her, losing his footing in the churning water before righting himself. Together, he and Camilla grabbed the old man, hauling him to safety.

Despite their heroics, Sean and Camilla were shaken by the devastation surrounding them. Homes washed away, belongings scattered, animals fighting the impossible currents. So much loss and destruction. Camilla blinked back tears as the body of a small dog rushed past her in the flowing water.

"It's not your fault." Sean's gentle words helped ease her pained expression. "You've saved so many already."

"It's not enough." Camilla's voice broke.

He squeezed her shoulder. "Our best is all we have to offer."

Sean steadied himself as Betts and Elmer Jones, clutching each other, made their way outside. They'd stayed inside McCall's restaurant until safety required them to leave.

The floodwaters churned angrily around them, but Sean, and another man he didn't know, kept them on course toward higher ground. Betts refused to let go of her husband's hand, jaw set in determination.

"Just a little farther to the church," Sean called over the roar of the water. "We'll be there soon."

Betts leaned forward, squeezing Sean's shoulder. "Thank you for coming for us."

"I can't let the best hot chocolate maker and her husband get swept out of town."

As they rounded a bend, their breaths caught. Ahead, the church loomed, already partway submerged. The doors and windows were smashed open, the cross atop the steeple askew.

Betts gasped. "Oh no..."

"We'll check the community building behind the church. It's on higher ground."

Sean maneuvered them behind the church, finding the community building barely touched by the flood. "Let's get you folks inside out of this rain."

They stomped up the steps to shove the door open. The inside was eerily silent. Though not as bad as the church, the building used for parties and community events had a slight amount of water covering the floor.

"We're lucky the fireplace was elevated with a hearth," Sean said.. "We'll start a fire to get you warm."

He gathered wood from a stack on the hearth while Betts found a blanket, wrapping it around her husband. Returning to the storage cupboard, she grabbed two more, handing one to Sean.

"Save it, Betts. I'll be bringing additional people who'll need it more than me."

The fire soon blazed, its light and warmth chasing away the chill. Betts and Elmer huddled together, taking comfort in one another as the flood raged on outside.

Chapter Twenty-One

Sean and Camilla stood on the edge of town a few days later, taking in the destruction caused by the flood. Mud-clogged streets were littered with debris. Collapsed buildings, missing roofs and walls. A doll floating face down along a fence.

She shuddered, tears welling in her eyes. He wrapped a comforting arm around her shoulders.

"I know it seems hopeless now. The town will rebuild. We'll all be stronger than before."

She managed a nod, drawing strength from his reassuring presence.

In the distance, they heard hammering. Townspeople were already patching roofs, salvaging lumber, clearing paths. Their perseverance sparked something in Sean and Camilla.

"Come on." Sean rolled up his sleeves. "Let's see what we can do."

They joined the efforts, hauling soggy furniture from waterlogged homes. Arms full, Camilla carried soaked clothing, already smelling of mildew and rancid creek water, to a barrel outside.

Around them, neighbors embraced, grateful to be alive. Though they'd lost much, their community still stood.

By nightfall, the streets almost looked passable again. Lanterns glowed in windows where families took refuge. The town was still bleeding but no longer broken.

As dusk settled over the ravaged town, Sean and Camilla made their way to the church. A dozen people had worked all day to clear debris and dry the interior. Inside, candles flickered, casting a welcoming glow over the pews. Quiet murmurs echoed through the sanctuary as people gathered to pray and find comfort.

Reverend Paige stood among them, his face etched with sorrow and fatigue. Even so, his voice rang out clear and true.

"My friends, we have suffered a great tragedy. Our town lies in ruins, our homes destroyed, our loved ones lost." He paused, eyes glistening. "We, however, are not lost. Here, in this house of God, we are together."

Sean slipped his arm around Camilla, both drawing and giving strength.

"Though the floodwaters have receded, the road ahead remains difficult," the reverend continued. "We will mourn, for we have much to mourn. But we will also rebuild. Splendor will rise again because of the spirit and resilience of its people."

Sean scanned those present, most had lived in Splendor for years. Every person had lost a friend or loved one. There would be more heartache and backbreaking work in the days to come. Tonight, huddled together under the church's rafters, the people of Splendor felt the first stirrings of healing.

As the reverend's final words echoed through the church, Sean took Camilla's hand, leading her outside into the cool night air. They walked in silence through the streets, the full moon illuminating the destruction surrounding them.

Shattered beams, crumbled brick walls, overturned wagons. It was difficult for Sean to reconcile the wreckage with the bustling town he'd known only days before. He glanced at Camilla and saw the same sorrow mirrored in her eyes, along with so many questions.

"How will we ever rebuild? How will the people make it through the loss?"

"The same way we survived the flood," he answered. "It won't be easy, but we'll do it one day at a time, one brick at a time."

She nodded, some of the spark returning to her eyes. "You're right. We should start planning immediately. There's so much to do..."

They made their way through the muddy streets, skirting overturned wagons and broken front windows. All around them was the evidence of the flood's devastation. Splintered wood, scattered belongings, childrens' toys.

There were also signs of life amidst the wreckage. Smoke curled from a few chimneys. Voices called out as people searched for loved ones. The sound of hammers.

As they walked, Camilla considered where to establish a shelter and distribution center for food and supplies. Her mind churned with ideas for organizing work crews to clear debris and reconstruct buildings. The first step would be to meet with the women who'd befriended her.

Camilla strode down the street the following morning, her jaw set with determination. She was on a mission to establish an emergency shelter and distribution center for the many left destitute by the recent flooding. Though the fine silk dresses in her wardrobe marked her as a lady of means, she was no helpless socialite.

Sean emerged from helping Stan Petermann in the general store, falling into step beside her. "You're in a hurry. Where to?"

"To speak with my friends."

Sean nodded. "About organizing a shelter?"

"Correct. And a way to distribute donations of food and clothing."

He grasped her hand. "Martha and Cole need help at the orphanage right now. I'll lend them a hand and make sure the children are cared for, so you can focus on the rest of the town."

She stopped, turning toward him. "Thank you. If

women of this town band together, I know we can make a difference." She kissed his cheek, her mind already racing ahead to the work yet to be done.

Camilla's first stop was the boardinghouse owned by Suzanne and Nick Barnett. The woman's eyes lit up when Camilla shared her idea for an emergency shelter and distribution center.

"Nick and I were discussing something similar last night. It's a wonderful idea." Suzanne set aside the loaf of bread she'd been kneading. "So many families lost everything in the flood. The men are already banding together to rebuild. There's no reason the women can't organize to help in other ways."

Camilla smiled, glad to have Suzanne's support. She received a similar response from each of her other friends.

Lena jumped at the idea. "I'd suggest an emergency meeting first thing tomorrow. I'll spread the word in case there are others who'd like to help. "

Camilla arrived early at the community building, ready to discuss plans for the emergency shelter. She and the other women were about to start their meeting when the front doors swung open.

In swept an elegant woman in a feathered hat and silk gown. Ruby Walsh, the owner of Ruby's Grand Palace saloon, had arrived. Her sharp eyes swept the room.

"Well, don't let me interrupt. I heard about the meeting and thought I'd offer my services."

Camilla blinked in surprise as Ruby settled herself at the table. Before she could respond, a few more women who'd learned of the meeting entered, taking seats. Gratified at the response, she called the meeting to order.

"As you all know, many families lost everything in the flood. I propose we establish an emergency shelter for them."

"The Grand Palace has plenty of room, plus cots and blankets," Ruby offered. "We'll be ready to take in people later this morning."

"Excellent," said Camilla.

Suggestions flew fast and furious. A communal kitchen, activities for children, and washing lines. Camilla could hardly contain her smile.

"These are wonderful ideas," she said.

"We need a distribution center for donations of food, clothing, and other supplies," Lena said. "I think right here in the community building would work well for that purpose."

The others murmured in agreement.

"We can use the back room here to store donations as they come in," suggested Suzanne.

"And we'll need volunteers to hand out supplies and keep things organized," added Olivia McCord.

"I can spare some staff to lend a hand," offered

Ruby. Though some in town looked down on her saloon, the woman had a generous spirit beneath her flashy exterior.

The next hour was spent hammering out further details, such as setting up a schedule for donations and distribution times, designating volunteers for various tasks, and figuring out how to best spread the word about their efforts.

As the meeting drew to a close, Camilla felt deeply moved by the generosity she'd witnessed. "We've accomplished much today. There is still more work to be done. I know the town can count on your continued support in the days ahead."

A chorus of assent met her words. One by one, the women filed out of the hall, some stopping to talk to Camilla. She saw determination shining in each face. The women were energized by their shared purpose.

Sean arrived back at the veterinary clinic late in the afternoon, eager to share with Camilla the progress made at the orphanage. Together, with Cole, Martha, Morgan Wheeler, and the children, they'd cleared debris, assessed damages, and begun repairs. They were fortunate the upstairs hadn't suffered the same damage as the first floor. At least the children had a place to sleep and continue classes.

As he entered the clinic, Sean found Camilla

sweeping the floors in an attempt to rid the house of the remaining water. Though his house had missed the worst of the flooding, her house had been spared without any damage. It was where he'd sprawled out on the sofa, her in the bedroom, to catch a few hours of sleep. Turning at the sound of his footsteps, she smiled.

"Sean, I have such good news. We're setting up an emergency shelter at the Grand Palace and a distribution center in the community hall. People without places to go are already arriving at Ruby's."

She described the productive meeting, her voice brimming with hope and pride. Sean listened intently, admiration growing with every detail.

"That's wonderful, Camilla. You've accomplished a great deal today."

He recounted the progress at the orphanage, and Camilla's smile broadened. She squeezed Sean's hand, reveling in his warm strength.

"Once word spreads, I believe others will offer help to restore the orphanage," Sean continued.

"We'll ask Martha to make a list of what they'll need. There's no reason we can't request supplies for the orphanage while we're collecting items for the town."

Sean drew her into his arms for a kiss. Lifting his head, he looked into her eyes. "I like the way you think, Miss Santori."

Camilla rose early the next morning, excitement coursing through her. Arriving at Ruby's, she found Lena and Suzanne already there, brewing coffee and laying out breakfast foods donated by the Eagle's Nest.

"Morning," Suzanne called out. "Ruby's girls had this place all ready when Lena and I arrived. There are a few families and some singles who've moved in. There's not much for us to do. I'd suggest we concentrate on collecting donations for distribution at the community building. There are enough volunteers here to take over for us."

Within half an hour, the women had changed locations, joining others to set up the distribution of donated goods. Word had spread fast. There were already piles of clothing, and a crate of canned goods from Stan Petermann.

Ruby sauntered in, followed by two of her girls. "We brought some more blankets and lanterns." She deposited her load near the back room. "What needs doing first?"

As more volunteers trickled in, Camilla organized work details. The morning passed quickly as the women scrubbed floors, accepted donations, and took inventory of supplies. Laughter and conversation mingled with the sounds of labor.

Around noon, Gabe swung by with a wagonload of lumber donated by Silas Jenks. "He sends his regards," Gabe told Lena, brushing a kiss across his wife's cheek. "Anything else you need, let me know."

Across the room, Ruby and Camilla sorted donations into piles. "Whoever thought someone like me would be helping the church women," Ruby mused. "Guess some might faint straight away at the sight."

Camilla smiled up at her. "Folks can surprise you. I know I misjudged you, Ruby. I'm thankful you're here."

Ruby grinned as she set a stack of men's trousers to the side. "Well, takes all kinds to make a town. We'd best learn to work together if we aim to get through this."

Chapter Twenty-Two

The morning sun cast its golden glow across the recovering town of Splendor as Sean and Camilla readied themselves for a brief respite from the chaos. She hummed to herself while packing a simple picnic of cold chicken, slices of bread, and dried fruit.

Her thoughts drifted to the handsome veterinarian who'd come to mean so much to her in these past harrowing weeks.

Sean had already saddled their horses, which he'd tied to a post outside her house. A smile played on his lips in anticipation of the day ahead with Camilla.

She appeared on the front porch, holding out the prepared lunch packed in two cloth pouches. Taking them from her, he slipped them into his saddlebags.

"Shall we?" Sean extended his hand, helping her mount the chestnut mare. They rode next to each other, the landscape around them beginning to show signs of rebirth.

After a time, Sean motioned for them to stop at a lookout off the trail. Before them sprawled the vista of Splendor.

"Look how far the town has come already."

Camilla gazed at the incredible sight before her, then back at Sean.

"It's been an amazing experience. One I hope to never encounter again."

He knew what she meant, though experience had taught him disasters were part of living in the frontier.

They rode on in comfortable silence, enjoying each other's company and the beauty of the open countryside. The trail climbed gradually into the foothills, the town of Splendor and its ongoing reconstruction soon lost from view.

As the path narrowed, he led them single file through stands of ponderosa pine and flowering dogwood. Camilla breathed in the crisp mountain air, so different from the crowded streets of New York.

Rounding a bend, the meadow opened up before them into a sea of waving grasses and wildflowers, framed by the rugged peaks beyond. Birdsong filled the air as Sean helped her dismount.

"Mustang Meadow. It's magnificent." She shot him a look with one of the first genuine smiles he'd seen in much too long.

Sean nodded, drinking in the sight of her. How was it he'd come to care so much for this fascinating woman? She met his gaze, and in her eyes, he glimpsed the growing tenderness that mirrored his own.

They spread out the blanket and settled down to enjoy the meal. Their conversation flowed easily, punctuated by laughter, as two souls began entwining into one.

Sean opened the bottle of wine given to him by Michael at the St. James, and poured two glasses, handing one to Camilla.

"To new beginnings." He touched his glass to hers.

"To embracing the unexpected."

They sipped, the sweet wine mingling with the fruit flavor still on their tongues.

"Do you ever wonder how we got here?" Sean asked. "If someone had told me a few months ago I'd be picnicking with a sophisticated New York heiress, I'd have said they were plumb loco."

She laughed, the sound rippling over the meadow. "The vagaries of fate can be quite surprising. I certainly didn't travel out west seeking romance." Her tone grew more serious. "But I'm thankful our paths crossed when they did."

Sean nodded, holding her gaze. "So am I."

A relaxed silence settled between them as they contemplated the improbable series of events that had led to this moment. The trilling of songbirds accentuated the quiet.

Laying back on the blanket, her eyes drifted shut. Sean's calming presence lulled her into peaceful rest.

As she dozed off, he studied her graceful features, her chest rising and falling in a steady rhythm. He reclined next to her, watching the clouds drift across the azure sky. Her nearness stirred feelings he'd long kept buried. Turning his head, he studied her serene face.

"Camilla?"

Her eyes fluttered open to meet his gaze.

"I know we come from different worlds, with different expectations placed on us. From the moment I first saw you, I felt an unexplainable connection."

She propped herself up on one elbow, her expression intent. "I felt it, too, though it frightened me at first. I was taught to prize pedigree and status. I've discovered that's not who I am. Not truly."

He reached out, drawing a finger down her cheek. "There's more to life than society's constraints. Don't you think?"

"I do." She took hold of Sean's rough, calloused hand.

Sean interlaced his fingers with hers. Leaning closer, he brought his lips to Camilla's in a tender kiss. As they parted, she saw her own exhilaration reflected in his eyes.

"I want this, Sean," she whispered. "I want to build a life with you, no matter the cost."

He grinned. "Is that a proposal?"

Her eyes lit with mischief. "It could be."

Sean cupped her cheek, his rough fingers igniting sparks along her skin. "It won't be easy, building a life in this untamed land. I believe together, we're strong enough to weather any storm."

"I believe the same."

He pulled her close once more. "Then it's settled. We face the future side by side, come what may." Brushing a kiss across her lips, he pulled back, touching his forehead to hers.

"I love you, Camilla. Marry me."

"And I love you." She settled her mouth over his for a brief kiss. Pulling back, she gazed into his beautiful emerald green eyes. "I'd be honored to be your wife."

The beaming smiles they exchanged sealed their commitment at the same time a light rain began to fall.

Reluctantly, they packed and mounted their horses for their return to Splendor.

"I wish we could stay here forever," she said in a wistful voice.

Sean reached for her hand, bringing it to his lips for a tender kiss before urging his horse forward.

The sun cast golden light over the landscape as they descended the hillside. They rode next to each other, stealing glances at each other the entire way.

Camilla met his gaze. "We should tell Cole and Martha first."

"Agreed."

Their hands found each other again, bridging the space between their mounts. The trail leveled out as Splendor came into view. As they approached the edges of town, they reluctantly let their clasped hands fall away.

At the livery, Cole awaited them, his sharp gaze taking in their mussed riding clothes. Understanding dawned on his features.

Camilla lifted her chin as a smile formed. "We intend to marry."

Cole studied them both, then broke into a grin. "Well, it's about time." He helped his sister to the ground, sweeping her into a fierce hug.

Over her shoulder, Cole met Sean's eyes. "Welcome to the family, Doc."

Epilogue

MacLaren Ranch
One month later...

The vigorous sounds of fiddle music and laughter filled the ranch as the wedding celebration continued. Sean MacLaren, dressed in his finest suit, a wide smile across his face, made his way through the crowd with his new bride, Camilla, on his arm.

"Thank you for celebrating with us today." Sean shook hands and clasped shoulders with guest after guest. Camilla glowed in her white lace gown, greeting each person by name, a testament to the effort she'd made to know the townsfolk.

He spotted his cousin Bram's tall frame across the way and steered his bride toward him. "Bram! We can't thank you enough for hosting our special day. It means the world to me and Camilla to have our wedding at your home."

Bram's stoic face cracked into a grin as he pulled Sean in for a bear hug. "Anything for my cousin and his bride." He turned to Camilla. "Welcome to the family, Camilla."

She leaned in, kissing his cheek. "Thank you for your hospitality. Everything is just wonderful."

When Bram excused himself, they continued through the sea of happy faces. She spotted her brother in deep discussion with Thane and steered them over.

"Cole!" She embraced him. "I'm so pleased you could stand being away from your duties for my wedding day."

Cole smiled down at his sister. "I wouldn't have missed it. You look radiant today." His eyes misted before he pulled himself together. "Now don't you worry about the town. Gabe left two of his best deputies to keep watch."

She turned to Thane. "Your ranch is incredible. You and Bram have built something wonderful here."

Thane inclined his head. "Many thanks, Camilla. May you and Sean have a long and happy life here."

As the newlyweds made their way back through the crowd, Sean squeezed Camilla's hand, his heart overflowing with love and optimism for their new life together.

Continuing to mingle with their guests, they exchanged greetings and expressions of thanks. As they moved through the crowd, a group of children ran by, laughing and shrieking with delight.

Little Emily Brandt nearly collided with Camilla, then stopped short and curtsied politely. "Sorry, Mrs. MacLaren," she said with an impish grin.

Camilla smiled down at the girl. "That's quite all right, Emily. It looks like you and your friends are having fun."

Emily's head bobbed with excitement. "We're playing tag. Do you and Mr. MacLaren want to play, too?"

Sean chuckled, ruffling the young girl's hair. "Maybe later. You enjoy the game for now."

As Emily scampered off to rejoin her friends, Sean and Camilla shared an amused smile.

Nearby, the enticing whiff of roasting meat, fresh baked bread, and fruit pies drifted through the air. Suzanne Barnett and other town ladies displayed their culinary creations on tables set near the edge of the gathering. Camilla's mouth watered at the sight of the delicious food.

"Remind me to thank the women," Sean murmured.

Camilla nodded. "They've all outdone themselves today."

He offered her his arm as the band struck up a slower tune. "May I have this dance, Mrs. MacLaren?"

Her eyes sparkled. "You may, Mr. MacLaren."

She placed her hand in the crook of his elbow, and he led her to the makeshift dance floor. Other couples were already twirling and stepping in time to the music.

They moved as one, their bodies swaying and feet gliding in graceful patterns across the floor. The steps came naturally, as if they'd danced together many times before.

As the song ended, Sean straightened and pulled Camilla close again, leaning in to place a tender kiss on her lips.

"I love you," he murmured, his voice thick with emotion.

"And I love you," she whispered in return.

Deputy Morgan Wheeler stood off to the side, observing the festivities. His gaze kept drifting to Amelia Newhall, her pretty auburn hair glistening in the late afternoon sun.

He'd admired her for some time now. Her kindness and dedication to the children was plain to see, and there was a spark in her hazel eyes that drew him in. He'd always been too shy to strike up more than a brief conversation when their paths crossed in town. The longest they'd been close to each other was on the wagon ride during the flood.

Today, seeing her in a simple blue calico dress that brought out the rosiness of her cheeks, Morgan felt a surge of resolve. This was a day for new beginnings. Perhaps it was time he made a beginning of his own.

Casually maneuvering through the crowd, he made his way to Amelia's side. "Good afternoon, Miss Newhall."

She looked up at him, tucking a stray curl behind her ear. "Oh. Good afternoon, Deputy."

"Please, call me Morgan."

"Only if you call me Amelia."

He chuckled. "It would be my pleasure...Amelia."

They stood in amicable silence for a few moments, both shy yet eager to continue the conversation.

"Are you enjoying the festivities?" Morgan asked at last.

"Oh, yes, everything is just lovely. Sean and Camilla seem so happy. It's wonderful to see."

"They do make a fine match." He hesitated for a moment. "I must say, you look lovely today, Amelia."

She glanced down, a blush rising on her fair cheeks. "You're too kind, Morgan."

Their eyes met and held for a long moment, a new understanding passing between them. Both could sense this was the beginning of something special.

For now, it was enough to stand together amidst the swirl of music and laughter. And the promise of what was to come.

Enjoying the **Redemption Mountain** books? Here's another series you might want to read.

MacLarens of Boundary Mountain historical western romance series.

If you want to keep current on all my preorders, new releases, and other happenings, sign up for my newsletter: http://www.shirleendavies.com/contact-me.html

A Note from Shirleen

Thank you for taking the time to read **Mustang Meadow**!

If you enjoyed it, please consider telling your friends or posting a short review. Word of mouth is an author's best friend and much appreciated.

I care about quality, so if you find something in error, please contact me via email at **shirleen@shirleendavies.com**

Books by Shirleen Davies

Historical Western Romances
Redemption Mountain
MacLarens of Fire Mountain Historical
MacLarens of Boundary Mountain

Contemporary Western Romance
Cowboys of Whistle Rock Ranch
MacLarens of Fire Mountain
Contemporary
Macklins of Whiskey Bend

Romantic Suspense
Eternal Brethren Military Romantic
Suspense
Peregrine Bay Romantic Suspense

Find all of my books at: http://www.
shirleendavies.com/books.html

About Shirleen

Shirleen Davies writes romance—historical and contemporary western romance, and romantic suspense. She grew up in Southern California, attended Oregon State University, and has degrees from San Diego State University and the University of Maryland. During the day she provides consulting services to small and mid-sized businesses. But her real passion is writing emotionally charged stories of flawed people who find redemption through love and acceptance. She now lives with her husband in a beautiful town in northern Arizona.

I love to hear from my readers.

Send me an email: shirleen@shirleendavies.com
Visit my Website: https://www.shirleendavies.com/
Sign up to be notified of New Releases: https://www.shirleendavies.com/contact/
Follow me on Amazon: http://www.amazon.com/author/shirleendavies
Follow me on BookBub: https://www.bookbub.com/authors/shirleen-davies

Other ways to connect with me:
Facebook Author Page: http://www.facebook.com/shirleendaviesauthor

Pinterest: http://pinterest.com/shirleendavies
Instagram:
https://www.instagram.com/shirleendavies_author/
TikTok: shirleendavies_author
Twitter: www.twitter.com/shirleendavies